IN THE WALLED CITY

In the
Walled City

STEWART O'NAN

GROVE PRESS
New York

for Trudy

Published by special arrangement with the University of Pittsburgh Press,
Pittsburgh, Pennsylvania

Published simultaneously in Canada
Printed in the United States of America

FIRST GROVE PRESS EDITION

Library of Congress Cataloging-in-Publication Data
O'Nan, Stewart, 1961–
    In the walled city / Stewart O'Nan.
        p. cm.
    Contents: The finger—The third of July—In the walled city—Calling—Winter haven—Finding Amy—Mr. Wu thinks—The doctor's sickness—The legion of superheroes—Steak—The big wheel—Econoline.
    ISBN 0-8021-3854-3 (pbk.)
    1. United States—Social life and customs—20th century—Fiction. I. Title.

PN3565.N316 15 2001
813'.54—dc21   2001040157

The Denis Johnson quote that appears on page vii is excerpted from his poem "The Honor" in *The Veil* (New York: Alfred A. Knopf, 1987).

Grateful acknowledgment is made to the following publications in which some of these stories first appeared: *Ascent* ("Econoline"); *Columbia* ("The Third of July"); *Jam To-Day* ("Mr. Wu Thinks"); *The Nebraska Review* ("Winter Haven"); *Northwest Review* ("The Finger"); *South Dakota Review* ("Calling"); and *The Threepenny Review* ("Steak").

I'd also like to acknowledge, first, the Cornell University MFA program for giving me both the time to write and a community of interested readers. I'd like to thank especially Stephanie Vaughn and Michael Koch, Lamar Herrin, Dan McCall, Jim McConkey, and Lorrie Moore, all of whom shared their time and experience generously. Thanks also to everyone who read these stories in and out of workshop, including my faithful readers whose comments helped shape the collection: Neil Plakcy, Manette Ansay, Tim Melley, and Jennie Cornell. Thanks, too, to Jen Hill and Larry Cantera, Deidre Pope, Juni Diaz, Michael Friedman, Peter Landesman, Elizabeth Graver, Paul Cody and Liz Holmes, Craig Triplett, Kim Dionis, Stu Shephard, Ed Hardy and Tamar Katz, Bob Fecho, Glenna and Kathy McKenzie, Kyna Taylor, Burlin Barr and Linda Wentworth, Joe Martin and Nancy Couto, John Landretti, Lisa Neville, the Southwicks and O'Nans, and, of course, Buck Schaefer. Without your talent, patience, and support, this book would not exist. And belated thanks to all who helped me get started and pointed me in the right direction: Daniel and Audrey Curley, Bill Roberson, Russell Banks, Scott Sommer, and David Bradley. Finally, thanks to Tobias Wolff for choosing my manuscript and to Fred Hetzel, Ed Ochester, Beth Detwiler, Peter Oresick, and everyone at Pitt for turning it into a book.

Grove Press
841 Broadway
New York, NY 10003

01 02 03 04   10 9 8 7 6 5 4 3 2 1

Contents

People will tell you that it's awful
to see facts eat our dreams, our presumptions,
but they're wrong. It is an honor
to learn to replace one hope with another.

— Denis Johnson

IN THE WALLED CITY

The Finger

Sundays, Carter saw his wife and baby. It was not his decision and not Diane's either, they just went along with it. There was nothing legal between them. They'd been separated barely a year, and if they still bristled face-to-face, distance had given him back some of his lost fondness.

Carter knew she was seeing people, but compared with their years together—the rhythm of apartments and, in those fat and sunny years, bungalows—a few dinner dates with slicked-up slobs from work didn't worry him. Sometimes when Diane was hurting for cash, Carter would take the bus over to Bay Shore after work and put an envelope in their mailbox. He was making the best money of his life at the landfill, and she had to pay the babysitter, she needed to buy food. Carter felt responsible in a way he hadn't when they were together.

This Sunday he was walking back from the bus stop along William Floyd Parkway toward his complex—at peace for having fulfilled his obligations—when a car shot by him with a man hanging out the passenger side window. He was maybe a little younger than himself, dark, with a DI and a pointed beard. Very clearly, the man called to Carter, "Fuck you," and gave him the finger, pumping his whole arm for emphasis. Carter stopped walking. The car—a big, brown LTD with New York plates—made the light at Montauk Highway, rumbled over the railroad tracks, and sped away down the Floyd toward the beach.

"Drunk," Carter said, and kept walking along the berm. It was Sunday, mild, late April, a few hours of light left. He debated buying a quart of Miller at the Dairy Barn and brown-bagging it on

3

the beach. He needed some release after the effort of keeping the peace with his wife all afternoon. Jessie was sick, napping late, and he and Diane had sat in the kitchen, pretending to be civil, unscathed. She ran water for coffee, and he noticed the faucet leaked around the base.

"It's not your problem," she said.

"It's a two-dollar part. It'll take me five minutes."

She talked about gardening; she did every year but never planted anything.

"You don't like green pepper," he reminded her.

"I can get to like it. I'm going to give most of them to Mrs. Contas."

"What else?" he asked, because he liked to see her make plans. It was something he was no good at, and partly why he'd fallen for her. Her original plan was to get her circuit board certificate from the SUNY extension and work at Grumman's; then he could quit and go back to school full time. Late nights, sweeping the laundromat, Carter would stop amid the warm tumbling of the dryers and think of her taking notes, cross-legged, imagining in a few years he'd be there. He had wanted — and still wanted — to be a physical therapist. A year before their marriage, he'd laid down his bike in the rain and shattered a knee. When the doctors cut the cast off, the leg was grayish-yellow and half the size of the other, the quad jelly. He couldn't bend the knee and thought he'd never be the same. He wanted to be like the people who saved him.

The guy with the beard had leaned out, made a real effort, Carter thought. There was no one around him, no one else walking the sandy shoulder. He wondered, as cars shot by in hot waves of exhaust, if the man had mistaken him for someone he knew. Or if in some crummy part of his life he had actually known the man — had deserved maybe more than the finger. Maybe right now the LTD was doubling back. He kept an eye on the oncoming traffic. Probably just a joke, high spirits. Why would anyone wish that on another?

The Finger

He and Diane hadn't been sleeping together for a few weeks when she told him she was pregnant. Their plans had fallen through and they were living off his father — money Carter had vowed he'd never accept. He'd been seeing an ex-friend of hers, and the way he flaunted his own coldness, he expected Diane would find someone — a guy from work, a nice guy, he didn't want to know. He had imagined it again and again, but a baby was stupid. He wanted to think it was his. Diane didn't.

Against his father's urging, Carter moved out east on the Island where it was cheaper. He had a one-bedroom in a failed retirement complex. A lot of the original tenants were still there, getting by on assistance. It was quiet, if a little rundown.

If he could buy a quart with just the change in his pockets, he would. It was a game he couldn't really lose. He was short a quarter but decided to splurge anyway. It was Sunday, he wasn't doing anything. He bought two and made sure to chat up the clerk, who looked like a regular guy, a good guy, Carter thought, maybe had a family. The Dairy Barn was a drive-thru; the man was probably lonely.

How the hell would he know?

The weather brought the oldsters out. On the lawn in front of his building, Mr. Katz and a guy Carter knew from the laundry room sat in folding chairs, bundled up. Mr. Katz had a Mets cap on to keep the sun out of his eyes. They were both holding dollar bills.

"Here's my friend Carter. Tell Manny here it is impossible to dig up a prehistoric elephant — we're talking a couple billion years old here — and eat it like it's leftovers. Will you tell him that?"

"Carter?" Manny said, "Carter, you've heard of the woolly mammoth, is that right? So you know they find them frozen in the ice. In the Arctic. What I'm saying is, these archeologists who find them find them totally preserved."

"Like a big freezer, he's saying."

"And when they taste the meat it's fresh like from the butcher. They eat it up, throw a picnic right there in the Arctic."

"I never heard that," Carter said.

"See? The man won't lie." Mr. Katz reached for the dollar but Manny pulled his hand away.

"I'm not talking Ripley's here, this is the *National Geographic,* for God's sake."

"It might be," Carter said, "I just never saw it."

"That doesn't prove anything."

"What do you want," Mr. Katz said, "the *World Book Encyclopedia?*"

"You guys want to drink some beer?"

"Gives me gas," Mr. Katz said.

"With my stomach?" Manny said.

"Mr. Woolly Mammoth," Mr. Katz said, "Mr. Picnic-on-the-Tundra."

"Carter," Manny said, "remind me never to ask you anything ever again."

Inside, Carter left his lights off, sitting in a square of sun, moving his chair as the beer dwindled. He imagined himself at the beach, the failing light bronzing the water. It was probably cold; besides, it was a long walk. He could not stop thinking about the guy with the beard, how he stuck his upper half out to yell at him. Carter was probably lucky they hadn't come back for him with baseball bats. Who was driving? Diane could have easily beaten him out there, the car her boyfriend's. Looked like her type — psychotic. She swore she wasn't sleeping with anyone, but he knew she was saying it for him, for the money. He did not want to believe his cynicism anymore; he was tired of living for himself, and liked to think the chill between them would — like everything of importance, unspoken, an understanding beyond argument — miraculously thaw. Every time he went over to the old place he had the urge to stay the night, stay the next day and on and on, as if nothing had changed. She never offered, he never asked.

The room was going dark, the beer dregs. He went to his footlocker and made sure he had clothes for tomorrow. At work they provided jumpsuits, but Carter always worried that the smell of the garbage was seeping into his skin, like a virus. Since his father had finagled the job for him, he'd slowly lost his sense of smell. In the beginning he wore the mask they gave him, but it didn't work and none of the others wore theirs. On the bus sometimes people stayed away from him; other days they pressed right into his pits. If he stank he wasn't able to tell, but every time he did laundry he'd sniff and sniff, unsure.

Diane never said anything. She knew his father had gotten him the job after they'd broken up. At first Carter had hated him for it, but he no longer minded the job. He liked sitting high up in the Cat's glassed-in cab, packing and grading the great mounds of trash, the gulls thick and wheeling above. The fill was the highest point for miles, and on a clear day he could see the trawlers rocking far off Fire Island. Best, he knew the job was temporary. Not because he could afford to quit, but because he could not imagine himself working in the heat and stink for more than a few years.

He laid out his clothes for tomorrow, then made himself dinner—a fried egg sandwich washed down with Hi-C out of the big cold can. It disgusted and dismayed him. He told himself this was all temporary.

He called Diane.

"What do you want?" she answered.

"I just wanted to know you were all right."

"I'm all right."

"I had a good time today."

"Right. Look, we're eating."

"We."

"Me and Jess," she said as if he'd said something absurd. "I've got to go."

"Listen," Carter said, "I had this thing happen to me today."

"You're drinking. Jesus, I can smell it on you from here."

"Just beer, I swear it."

"I'll see you next Sunday," she said, and hung up.

By nine everyone in his building was in bed. Carter listened to the kids from the other buildings playing flashlight tag, private planes landing at Brookhaven Airport, and, beneath it all, the steady wash of cars on the Floyd. He couldn't wait to fall asleep, to wake up.

He rode the Cat, thinking of Sunday, far off and bright as the island sky. The wind was up, riffling skeins of plastic caught in the razor wire. Monday was white-items day, neighborhood contractors bringing in truckloads of doorless refrigerators and stoves and washers and dryers, halved kitchen tables and matching chairs, broken-backed couches, ripped Barcaloungers. Vernon, the manager, set aside the nicer pieces behind his trailer — first come first serve. Anything left on Friday got tossed. Carter's apartment was furnished with such junk, most of it beyond his means.

At break Lorena said there was a nice sectional he might like, and they took their coffees around back. Lorena knew his father from the water authority, and looked after Carter as if he were helpless. Carter appreciated it.

The sectional was tan and had five pieces including a curve, across which lay a plate-sized wine stain. Lorena swiped at the cushions and sat down.

"It's nice," Carter said, "but I don't have the room."

"The stain. Don't feel pressured. If you can't use it, my niece might. Did you look at the dresser with the nice handles?"

It was red oak, a little nicked but better than the pressboard one he had at home, found here last August. He could strip it and stain it.

"I don't know," he said, "I've got enough stuff already."

"Maybe Diane could use it."

"Maybe," he said. "Sure, hey, what the hey."

Lorena gave him a ride home with the dresser wrapped in an old army blanket, legs sticking out of the trunk. The Dairy Mart passed. Mr. Katz supervised them getting it up the stairs and into Carter's apartment.

"It was a mastodon," Mr. Katz said after Lorena had left.

"What?"

"Your woolly mammoth, it was a mastodon. Manny got this book from the library. These guys picked the thing apart like a nice whitefish. They even got a picture of it."

"What are you telling me for?" Carter asked.

"Mr. Irritable here. I thought you were interested. A stick of wood is more interesting, is that it?"

"It's for my wife." He had it on an island of newspaper in the living room. Mr. Katz was on the couch, his cane between his legs.

"What for?"

"It's a gift." He opened the can of stripper.

"What do you want to do that for? Buy her a nice dress or something, take her out to dinner." He took out a handkerchief and held it to his nose. "Are you supposed to be doing this indoors?"

Carter opened a window.

"Forget it," Mr. Katz said, and hobbled to the door. "Call me when she dumps you again."

"Leave it open," Carter said.

He brought a wobbly floor lamp over and took off the shade so he could see what he was doing. He soaked a pad of steel wool with stripper and rubbed along the grain. The stain came off gummy, dying his fingers like nicotine. He skipped dinner, scouring the scrolled legs, the ball-and-claw feet. The steel wool wore down and pricked his fingers, the stripper burned. Midnight, groggy from the fumes, he could see it was going to work. He stood back, admiring the bare whorls. The complex was dark, silent; he closed his door. Around two he ran out of steel wool and quit for the night. The stain wouldn't come off his fingers, even using Goop. Hours later, he got out of bed and closed the window.

He woke up with a crushing headache. It poured, fog sitting over the sea. The first two hours not a single truck showed. Only pros ran in the rain. He sat in his cab with the heater up, listening to the roof drumming, the wipers slishing. Gulls stood in flocks, puffed for warmth. He thought of the dresser sitting in his dark apartment, how foolish he was to think it would change things.

Right at break, a town truck climbed the hill, its lights on, stacks smoking. Lorena radioed him that he could go back to the trailer.

"You go," he said. "I'll take it."

"Sure?" she said.

The truck backed to the wall of trash, raised its bed, and began inching out, laying a long swath of garbage. Carter dropped his blade, throttled up, and headed for the pile. The truck lowered its bed and its gate banged shut. The driver gave Carter a flash of his high beams, which Carter returned. As they passed, the driver stuck his arm out the window and waved. Carter did not know him but waved back, confused but glad.

Walking back from the bus, he stopped at the Odd Lot to pick up some steel wool. It was a cheap store, piled to the ceiling with flimsy knotted pine and overpriced hardware from Taiwan that other stores couldn't sell. The local contractors drove the twenty miles to the Pergament in Bohemia; here were only men like himself, husbands looking for a length of downspout or tube of caulking to keep the house together until the next crisis, whatever the cost. They stalked the aisles searching for one item, and when they found it strode to the checkout, paid in cash, and were out the door, in the car, and away. Carter knew the routine; he liked working with his hands. When the screen door came apart or the tiles in the shower stall began dropping, he would hop in the Valiant before Diane had a chance to call the problem to his attention and streak to the Pergament. He never remembered to ask for a receipt, but he did good work, and only the rare landlord argued.

Carter was not familiar with the Odd Lot, and wandered through the aisles trying to discover some logic in the arrangement of pyramids of lacquer, baskets of flashlight batteries, and bins of drywall nails. All of it seemed to be on sale, each price jotted in the white center of the same fluorescent red explosion. He found a stretch of paint cans, above it a wall of brushes and rollers, but no scrapers or sandpaper, no steel wool. The woman at the counter said she didn't remember any. Considering it a dead issue, she picked a microphone from its wall mount, and her voice burst godlike from the ceiling: "Fred, front, Fred."

Fred took him back to the paint cans and gave up. "We should be seeing some next week," he said, doubtful.

The two lawn chairs Mr. Katz and Manny were in the other day sat on the front lawn, getting rained on. Carter took his beer inside and set it on the stairs, went back out, folded the chairs and hauled them in, one in each hand.

The dresser was waiting for him when he opened the door. He took off his coat by the closet, careful not to drip on the raw wood. He tried to drink his beer by the window, looking out on the matted patch the kids adapted to whatever they were playing, but the dresser lurked behind him, and he moved to the kitchen. He ate some questionable leftover chicken and, gathering himself for tomorrow—sunny, the weather said—buried himself under the covers and dreamed of the Pergament's bright aisles.

It was eighty the next morning; green shoots and tiny flowers fringed the gray mounds. Home owners showed up in pickups and rental trucks, dropped off their attic or basement clutter, then spun and dug their rear wheels into the loose dust. Far below at the base of the fill, a line of trucks formed at the scales, running along the access road, out the entrance, and down the county road in both directions. Carter and Lorena worked through break. It was the kind of day Carter loved. He unzipped his jumpsuit to the waist, peeled off the top and his T-shirt, and drove barechested, the sweat streaming down his arms. The sun climbed, then seemed to linger, high, and the afternoon flew. Even the crushed gulls couldn't stop him whistling.

At the Pergament he didn't bother with a cart. The automatic doors welcomed him, and he strode to the paint aisle, scanned the bins, and found what he needed. He did a quick double check to make sure he was getting the best price, reread the label to make sure there was no mistake, and, sure of the rightness of the future and the goodness of humanity, strode toward the congested checkout. He chose the shortest line, and after browsing the display of ChapStick and correction fluid and pine tree air fresheners, peeked over at the other customers.

In the next lane a pudgy, balding man about his age had a baby facing him in his cart. With her huge blue eyes and chubby face, the baby looked like Jessie. It took Carter a second, struggling with the notion that all babies are cute, all babies in their newness look a little alike, to realize it was, in fact, his daughter.

The man looked past him, through him. His hair was brittle and frizzy around the bald spot, and he was wearing a neon tie-dyed T-shirt far too bright and tight for someone his age. Carter picked a Mickey Mouse night-light off the rack and pretended to scrutinize it. Mickey was dressed as a sorcerer, his cape and pointed hat emblazoned with moons and Saturns. The man had a few days gray growth of beard, and his face was subtly tinged yellow. The cart was empty; Jessie held the only thing they were going to buy—a molded, hard plastic ball for a Delta washerless faucet.

"Here we go," the man said, and pushed the cart up to the cashier.

"Is that all you want, honey?" the cashier asked, bending to Jessie and reading the code so she wouldn't have to take the package from her.

Carter's cashier—a stork of a boy with glasses and desperate acne—seemed to be having trouble. He stood staring at the register, a red telephone receiver jammed to his ear. Pinned to his apron was a button that said: Please Be Patient, I'm New.

The register in the next lane clicked and chimed and kicked out its drawer. The man paid, smiling, and rolled Carter's daughter away. Before they made the automatic doors, the man stopped before a tier of red-topped gumball machines, slipped a quarter out of his jeans and squatted, and, with Jessie directing, bought her something encased in a two-piece transparent plastic ball. She was still struggling to get it open when they disappeared outside.

Carter looked at the night-light, shook it in his hand as if deciding whether to toss it away, then slid it back on its peg.

After a turkey TV dinner, he worked fitfully, often stopping to sit on the couch with his arms crossed, sawdust itchy on his skin. His knee hurt; it was going to rain tomorrow. Mr. Katz and Manny were out on the lawn, the kids playing kick-the-can with his empty Hi-C, and Carter thought he could make up any lost time tomorrow. He turned his lights off and went out.

"How goes it, Romeo?" Mr. Katz asked. He and Manny were trading a hand telescope, looking up at the stars. The telescope was a cheap tin souvenir from Boston with stylized pictures of Plymouth Plantation and the USS *Constitution* printed on the body. Carter waited his turn.

"I think I see one," Manny said. "Is there one with a car?"

"Tell Carter about the shooting star we saw."

Manny leaned over to give Carter the telescope and his chair nearly tipped sideways. Carter couldn't smell anything, but the old man's eyes were in trouble. They'd been drinking, probably for some time, Carter thought. He drew the telescope to its length and looked up into the black. It actually worked—the stars jumped closer.

"What we saw was a meteor," Manny said, "that's what a shooting star is. And for those of you who don't know, this is the season for meteor showers."

"Who the hell doesn't know that?" Mr. Katz said. "You'd have to be a know-nothing not to know that."

"So I suppose you know where the largest recorded meteor landed?"

"Yonkers."

"Siberia," Manny said, "and it had so much radiation on it,

no one could live there. They're still not living there, that's how bad it is."

"What?" said Mr. Katz, "what are you telling me here?"

"God's honest truth," Manny said. "Turned all the plants into cannibals."

"Carter, tell Manny here he missed his medication."

"Siberia," Carter said, still looking up, the eyepiece cold on his socket.

"Yeah," Manny said.

"Sure," Carter said. "Who'd want to live there anyway?"

"Siberians," Mr. Katz said. "You wouldn't be talking like that to a roomful of Siberians."

"You're right," Carter said, "I wouldn't."

"Trade," Manny said, and jabbed a pint of blackberry brandy at him, spilling some. Carter tilted it back; in the distance, the Hi-C can clattered over the parking lot. "Olly Olly Olsen Free-O!" a girl called. Carter tipped the bottle back again.

"Keep it moving," Mr. Katz said.

"I'll get the next one," said Carter.

He paid for it the next morning, gloriously bright. His knee no longer ached, and he wanted to think a storm had skirted the island, passed roaring over the night sea. Lorena knew he was hurting, and let him rest when traffic was light. It was easily ninety; the flowers dried up and rotted like everything else. He drank soda from the machine, sat sweating in his cab, daubing his face with his balled shirt. On the bus, he took a chill from the air-conditioning, which the long walk down the shimmering Floyd melted out of him. He opened his door and stood there on the threshold, parched and wrung, before the unfinished gift.

He called, half expecting a man to answer.

"Carter," she said, disappointed, annoyed, "what is it?"

"Is this guy living with you?"

"That is none of your business," she said, "and I'm not going to discuss it with you—and not over the phone."

"You're sleeping with him, aren't you?"

"It doesn't matter."

"It doesn't matter," he said, and kicked the dresser so hard it rocked back. His toe felt broken, but he clung to the phone. "He fixed your faucet, he's living with you."

"Are you all right?" Diane asked.

"I'm fine!" Carter shouted, and slammed the receiver down before he began to sob outright.

The phone rang but he wouldn't pick it up. Later, he heard Mr. Katz and Manny in the hall. His lights were off; they'd think he was out. He moved from the couch to his bed and closed the bedroom door so he wouldn't have to see the dresser.

Maybe it was Friday, maybe it was the coming summer — the promise of ease, the luxury of sun — but the next morning, walking to the bus, Carter could not help but thrill to the lucky woodchuck skittering across all four lanes into the green ditch. His toe was not broken, only stoved, and she had called back, hadn't she? Sunday wasn't far. He hummed on the bus.

Rain walked in after lunch. He and Lorena were gabbing on the blower — she was going on a fishing charter tomorrow with his father — when she stopped and said, "Ten o'clock high." Far off, black and low, a shoal of clouds rolled shadows over the bay. His speaker crackled, the wind sent trash scattering like leaves, and rain pelted the dust.

"Sunday," he said. "All I need is a ride over; I can take the bus back myself."

"So what should I say to him?" Lorena asked. "Can I say you said hi?"

"Go ahead."

"What else?"

"I don't care," Carter said. "Tell him he was right and I was wrong."

"Seriously."

"Seriously," Carter said.

It was still pouring when Carter stepped off the bus. He had not brought an umbrella and got home soaked. He hung his clothes over the tub, put on his old laundromat uniform, ripped open the bag of steel wool, and went to work.

Mr. Katz and Manny stopped by a few minutes before dark and invited him out.

"I would but I've got to get this done."

"It's for his wife."

"I didn't know," Manny said.

"That's red oak," Mr. Katz said, and sat down on the couch.

"Black cherry," Manny said, sitting next to him.

"Next thing you'll be telling me it's cream soda."

"You guys want to help?" Carter asked.

"No," Mr. Katz said.

"You're doing fine by yourself," Manny said.

They left when he pried open the stain.

Saturday he put on a second coat, shellacked it once around dinner and again at midnight, and Sunday morning, with the help of Manny and Mr. Katz, he was standing beside the dresser in the parking lot when Lorena pulled up. The sky was high and bright, the beach traffic heavy early. It was the kind of Sunday, Carter thought, when you could believe in God as long as you didn't have to go to church. He wrapped the dresser in the army blanket and all four of them eased it into the trunk, upside down. They made a ceremony of seeing him off, as if he were on a suicide mission.

"Your father said he might give you a call," Lorena said on the way over.

"That would be good."

They kept to the right lane; other cars bombed by.

"He gives you a lot of credit, more than you think."

"Okay," Carter said.

In the foyer of his old place, he thanked Lorena and she wished him luck. He rang the bell under their mailbox. The dresser sud-

---

denly seemed small and fussy, and he thought the whole thing was a mistake — like the guy giving him the finger from the speeding car, not fate but coincidence.

The door clicked and buzzed, and Carter opened it and wedged a folded Chinese take-out flyer under it. He lifted the dresser, knees bent, hunched around the one end as if catching it, and maneuvered it through the door, sacrificing his hands rather than nick the wood. Inside, he put it down to close the door, then carried it halfway down the hall to the elevator. When he got the dresser to her door, he took a minute to catch his breath and comb his hair. He sniffed the good white shirt he had on, plucking the shoulder and holding it to his nose, then squared himself and the dresser with the door and knocked.

Diane had begun to frown automatically when she saw the dresser. She stepped out into the hall to look at it. "What is this?"

"It's a dresser," he said. "For you, or for Jessie when she's big enough."

"It's beautiful," she said, unsure, as if that might give him some advantage.

"It's yours. I found it at work and cleaned it up a little. I thought you might like it."

"Why?"

"I don't know, I just thought. Should I take it inside?"

They each took an end. She had them put it down in the living room, where Jessie was in her high chair, eating sliced bananas and watching cartoons. Carter tousled her fine hair — stiff with breakfast — and kissed her on the forehead.

"Let's go out," he said, "I feel like going out."

"As long as we're back by two," Diane said.

"What's at two?" he asked, then said, "Sure, we'll be back by two. Let's go to the boardwalk or the park, somewhere nice where we can enjoy this nice day."

"You pay for gas?"

"I get to drive?"

"Sure," she said, "knock yourself out."

"This is going to be great."

He hadn't driven a car in months. He put the window down and let his hair whip his face. They went to Eisenhower Park and he bought a kite. They flew it over the duck pond, letting Jessie feel the pull; then they went to Jones Beach and ate soft ice cream on the boardwalk and walked down to the surf in their good shoes. Diane held off telling him it was time to get back, and when she did she seemed sorry. He parked the Valiant and kissed them both good-bye, then went off to the bus stop, drunk with the sun and the sea.

The glow stayed with him on the bus, through the lush suburbs and potato fields, the day still promising. He bought two quarts and with his buddy the clerk weighed the odds of the Yanks getting out of the cellar.

Mr. Katz and Manny were waiting for him. They rose from their chairs and shook his hand and patted him on the back.

"You'll be out of here in a month," Mr. Katz said. "You'll forget us like we never existed."

"It's good," Manny said, punchy after two cups, "I wish you all the luck in the world, kid."

Carter let them have the second quart and went in to get some dinner. He was holding the fridge open, trying to decide if he should go out to celebrate, when the phone rang.

"I can't accept it," Diane said. "It's too expensive for a gift."

"It's yours."

"You've got to take it back."

"Is he there?" Carter said. "Because that's a gift, that's a gift to you and Jessie and has nothing to do with him."

"Cart, just take it back. I shouldn't have accepted it in the first place."

"That bald piece of shit. It's yours now, and I am not taking it back."

"Why do you have to be like this?" she said. "Why do you have to make everything so goddamn difficult?"

"It's not me, it's him."

"Are you going to take it back? It's a beautiful piece of furniture, and I'm grateful, but I can't accept it. Really, Carter, I can't."

"No," Carter said.

When Lorena asked him how things went, he said all right. It was a so-so day, a Monday, Carter didn't care. He took it out on the Cat, slamming deep into the mounds of trash, waves breaking over the cab.

"I'm sorry," Lorena said.

"Yeah, well," Carter said. "I was an idiot."

At lunch Vernon took them out back of the trailer. The dresser had come in on a white-item truck from Bay Shore. Vernon had spotted it before the driver could tip his load. Lorena inspected the damage. The top was scratched, one of the legs out of joint, but otherwise it was fine.

"I don't want to fix it," Carter said.

"Why not?"

"Because I already fixed it once."

"So?" she said.

He picked up one end of it. After a second she picked up the other. They carried it around the trailer and set it down in front of his Cat. He climbed into the cab, fired up and pulled forward, reducing the dresser to a nest of splinters sticking out from under the tread.

He jumped down to look.

"Now you're happy," Lorena said.

"Now I'm happy," he said.

"Why don't you take a half-day?" said Vernon.

"And do what?" Carter climbed up on the tread.

"Go on, I'll punch you out."

"He's all right," Lorena said.

It was another bright day, a good day to work. He turned off his radio and took every truck he could. By quitting time, Carter had satisfied his first rush of hatred. Disbelief set in momentarily, but with each run at the rotting trash, Carter knocked it back.

He was looking forward to getting drunk tonight, and when Lorena offered him a ride home, he weighed dealing with the people on the bus against making the walk to the Dairy Barn round-trip. They found their lunch buckets and punched out together. Outside, the dresser lay squashed where he'd rolled over it.

"What are you going to tell my father?" he asked.

"What do you want me to tell him?"

"I don't know," he said.

He felt better in the car. Lorena had air-conditioning, and he let it blow over him, watching the green world pass outside the window. He was ahead of himself a good half hour. Traffic on the Floyd wasn't bad yet. There were still kids riding their bikes, straggling home from band practice in packs.

"Your niece take that sectional?" he asked.

"It looks great too. She took most of the stain out, you can barely tell. How do people throw nice stuff like that away?"

Up ahead a man was walking the berm, dragging himself home after a day's work. He had on some sort of uniform, a light blue top and dark blue pants, like a gas-station attendant, and big, clunky boots. He slumped along, head down, carrying a brown paper bag in which Carter knew there was a quart of cold beer from the Dairy Barn. They shot past him. Carter did not turn to catch his face.

He did not get beer. Mr. Katz came over after dinner carrying a book. It was oversized and from the library, slipcovered in grimy cellophane.

"Here it is," he said, and opened the book to a photo of twenty or thirty men in parkas sitting around the ravaged corpse of an elephant. In the foreground stood a tripod from which hung a kettle; the men sat on stools with tin plates in their laps. They had all taken a break for the picture, and smiled wide, some holding up gnawed-on bones.

"Imagine getting someone to cater this?" Mr. Katz said.

The caption said there had been some diarrhea but no real

cases of food poisoning. A spring snow had cut off their supplies. It didn't say whose idea it was, and Carter went from face to face, trying to find among the gray eyes and smiles one man that crazy or brave. That first bite. Wouldn't it smell?

The next morning he took an early bus. Vernon was there, cleaning out the coffeepot. Lorena came in, surprised to see him. He asked if she could give him a ride home. "Sure," she said, "why?"

"Because I'm an idiot."

"Yeah?" she said.

"Yeah."

"Good," she said, and they took their coffees out back and strolled through the new arrivals, looking for something promising.

The Third of July

Lawson's first shot hit the lightning rod's middle insulator, shattering the milky ball and sending up a puff of glass. He was shooting with Danny's old BB gun, a rusted Daisy. It wouldn't kill the hawk, just make it think twice before going near his pigeons. He'd seen it coming back from his morning regimen in fifteen's water hazard and immediately knew what to do. If it hit prey the hawk would hang around till the whole flock was gone. He wasn't taking any chances. Ignoring his arthritis, Lawson pumped the action, aimed shakily and fired again. He tipped his cap back to see.

The hawk swiveled its head. It sat on the crossbar of a circular window under the peak of the barn roof. Only two dusty panes remained.

Lawson's elbow flared as he cocked the lever. "Damn rain," he said, and realizing it was not raining and had not for two weeks now, laughed. He felt his jacket's good pocket for his medicine. Forgot again. He rapped the open action against his thigh and drew a bead on the white-flecked breast. The post sight dipped and rose.

Inside the clubhouse, long ago the chicken coop, Mrs. May turned from the window, shaking her head. Here it was, eight in the morning, city crowd on the way, fairways practically tinder, and Mr. Lawson was fooling around. She opened the soda machine with her key ring, pressed a Fanta grape to her forehead and took a slug, then lit a Carlton with one burning in the ashtray and began arranging three-packs of Maxflis on the counter. It had been a bad summer — weren't they all since Mr. May passed to

23

glory?—and she was hoping today would be a good day. Three years ago the state had dammed Muddy Creek to make Lake Arthur and in the process wiped out a stretch of old Route 488, which passed by the course entrance. Now people took the state road, 422, out-of-towners sticking to Interstate 79. But today was July 3rd, people were everywhere. She dusted a lazy Susan rack of sunglasses and propped a cardboard display of red-white-and-blue sweatbands against the register. Outside, glass tinkled. "Give me strength," she said, and snapped on the PA.

"Mr. Lawson," a voice called from the trees. He looked up. "Do you know what today is?"

"Saturday," he hollered at the speaker.

"It is Saturday, Mr. Lawson, and around here Saturday is a workday. On workdays, we are supposed to work, not shoot up my windows, thank you very much." A shriek of feedback, a buzz, and the speaker went dead.

"I'm just trying to protect my birds," Lawson said. He said it again, and not receiving an answer, turned and looked for the hawk. It was gone.

He took the gun to the barn and put it back with Danny's things. They sat at right angles on an olive blanket draped over the hood of a red '67 GTO. In the tuck-and-rolled backseat lay another olive blanket and a pillow covered with blue-and-white ticking—in the frontseat, a neat stack of dungarees, another of baby blue Esso uniform shirts. Lawson placed the gun on the hood and inspected the bullet Danny had sent him from boot camp. It was as long as his big finger and looked like a tooth from a tiger or a whale or something. If he had a gun that shot something like that—that'd teach it. Lawson wrapped the bullet in a red bandana and laid it beside a stopped watch. He raked the floor around the car until his footprints were gone, hung his jacket on a nail, and, slowly, painfully, lifting one foot and then the other to each rung, climbed the ladder to the lower loft.

Before he threw off the tarp which covered the roost, he stood a second, listening to the pigeons coo and whir. Stunned by the light, they blinked as he counted them, poking a finger through the chicken wire.

They were all there except Martin Luther King. He was forty-five miles away, at Mr. Bottsie's in Homewood, getting ready for his maiden voyage. Bought from Mr. Bottsie as a present for Danny, Martin was the last of the original brood. He could be trusted to return. For the past eight Wednesdays, Mr. Bottsie had driven up Route 8 to Renfrew and taken Martin back toward Pittsburgh, setting him free five miles farther each time. If Mr. Bottsie let him go at three, as planned, Martin would be back for the slow time before supper. By then Lawson would have scared the hawk away.

First, though, he had business to take care of. Mrs. May was in no mood. He counted the pigeons again and replaced the tarp. They cackled in protest. "It's for your own good," he said, and climbed down painfully. He slid the barn door open, and after several noisy tries, fired up the tractor and roared out into the light.

Mrs. May intercepted him by the first tee. She was wearing a floral print blouse, black slacks, and graying sneakers. She carried a family-size can of Off which she waved above her head to get his attention. "Do the sprinklers first!" she yelled over the engine. Mr. Lawson nodded, waved, and slipped the tractor in gear. Creaking, the mower attachment threw fountains of dried grass. "The water!" she yelled, "the water!"

He left the tractor idling, got down and came over to her. "What'd you say?"

"The water," she said. When he looked back to the tractor and scratched the space between his nose and upper lip, she explained, "The grass cannot grow without water, now can it?"

"I cut first and then—"

"There's nothing to cut, Mr. Lawson. If you haven't noticed, we're in the middle of the worst drought in fifty years."

"Weatherman say that?"

"He doesn't have to." She squeezed the Off but the can didn't give. "Listen to me: do the sprinklers first. If we have to cut it later, I will personally cut it."

"But —"

"Sprinkle, Mr. Lawson, sprinkle."

"Yes, ma'am."

He swung the tractor around the first tee and headed back to the barn. Mrs. May sighed at the lopsided swath he left. He was her cross, of that there was no doubt. Him and his birds. And that car and those things from his boy, it wasn't natural. Then again, who in their right mind would take the job?

No one, she had found when she ran an ad in the *Butler Eagle*. It ran the whole of March and half of April before she realized she was wasting her money. When Reverend Smiley asked if anyone had room in their heart for a brother in less fortunate circumstances, willing to work for his keep, Mr. Lawson was not what she had in mind.

It was not that he was black or that he was a bad worker. He worked hard. The problem was that he was distracted. He worked on so many things at once that he never finished anything. Take the barn: since June one side had been whitewash, the other gray. And his car: every Wednesday after supper he backed it out and worked on the engine, gunning it, then ducking his head beneath the hood, but did he ever once drive it? Worse, none of these things seemed to bother him. While he calmly tinkered, the place was falling apart around her.

Her son Jonathan had been right, the place was too big for her alone. She should sell it and move into Pittsburgh, near him and that girl — what was her name? In any case, she saw no reason he should give up his engineering for some rundown golf course, even if it was a legacy. He had his own life, she understood that perfectly. She just thanked God Mr. May hadn't lived to see what his place had been reduced to. It would have killed him, sure as the lip cancer. She shook the Off until the little ball inside rattled, covered her mouth, and let loose a cloud. A bee blundered into the mist and fell to the picnic table. Mr. Lawson appeared from behind the clubhouse, flipping a wrench in the air and catching it with one hand. She thumbed the button and the bee drowned.

Lawson turned on the sprinklers on fairways one through seven. On eight, fighting a sticky valve, he mashed his pinky. He held his hand in his crotch and hopped. On eleven, in the crook of a dogleg, sheltered from the clubhouse by a bend of oak, he opened his flask and took a tug of peach brandy. The sweatband of his cap was brown, the back of his shirt soggy. He lay down in the shadows with the flask balanced on his chest and listened to the woods rustle and the hidden birds chirp. The sky shone a perfect drought blue, unbroken save a high, sailing speck.

Lawson ran across sixteen, up a hillock, and over the ninth green, switching the wrench from his left hand to his right and back. Keeping his eye on the hawk, he tripped over a baby fir and got up swearing.

In the parking lot, a man and a teenaged boy sat on the tailgate of a new station wagon, changing into their spikes. They both had white-blonde hair and squinty, tanned faces, and wore kelly green alligator shirts and khaki chinos. Mrs. May stood by, her hands clasped before her.

Lawson looked up. The hawk was sweeping circles, drawing them tighter and tighter as it climbed.

"Is there something, Mr. Lawson?"

"No, ma'am," he said, "hurt my hand's all." He flexed it.

"Oh my," she said, and took a step toward him to inspect it, but a wall of liquor knocked her back. She should have known. For her guests' sake she said, "Well, quick go and take care of yourself. We want the back nine to look as nice as the front."

"All I need's a piece of ice."

"There's plenty in the clubhouse," she said, but he was looking up at the sky as if it were about to storm. He stood with his chin in the air for a moment, then broke for the barn, tearing across the gravel. "That's Mr. Lawson," she explained to the man, who was shoving fluorescent green balls into his bag. "He's not all here all the time."

The man did not smile. He pointed to the browned course and asked, "Is it playable?"

"Till seven-thirty or sundown, whichever comes first."

The man bought two half-day passes at ten dollars each, the boy a thirty-nine-cent bag of tees. Mrs. May suggested they drive a few before teeing off. She said she wanted to let the fairways dry.

"What do you say to a bucket?" the man asked his son.

"I could hit one."

She lugged two buckets of red-striped range balls around the counter and led the man and his son around the barn to the range tee. The range was an overgrown meadow which sloped down to a creek, beyond which a loose barbed-wire fence held back clumps of oak and horse chestnut. Faded signs marked the yardage up to 300. Jonathan had painted them the last summer he came home from Penn State. As the man ground his tee into the dirt, Mrs. May told herself to remind Mr. Lawson to redo them.

The man let his son go first. His backswing was jerky, all elbows. The head of the driver scuffed the ground and the ball shot over the meadow, hooking to the left of the 100 sign and hopping once before settling in the high timothy.

"Try it a little slower," she offered.

"If you don't mind," the man said. He positioned himself behind the boy and placed his hands over the grip so they could both swing. The ball rose straight until it was lost in the bright sky, white on white, finally caroming high off the 150 sign. "Hold that front hip back," the man instructed, "that's where your power comes from." He knelt and held the boy's hip while he swung. "Feel that in your back?" When Mrs. May left they were both dropping them in at 200.

As she rounded the barn, she narrowly missed running into

---

an aluminum extension ladder. At the top, on his tiptoes, Mr. Lawson was reaching a square piece of plywood toward the window. He was well short of it. He climbed another rung and almost lost his balance, dropping a hammer which landed not five feet from her. When he looked down to see where it went, she beckoned him with a finger. It took him a few minutes to get down.

"What in the world," Mrs. May asked, "do you think you're doing?"

He pointed up. "Window's broken."

"That particular window has been broken the entire time you've worked here. Why would you pick today of all days to fix it?"

"I don't know, it needed fixed."

"No, Mr. Lawson, it needs to be fixed. Which it does, I agree with you there. However, right now we have more pressing concerns, such as the sprinkling, if you didn't remember." A car appeared on the access road, trailing dust. "When you're done turning the back nine on, turn the front nine off. We're going to be very busy today and I'm going to need your help. Do you understand?"

"Yes, ma'am," Lawson said, and she strode away. He waited for her to clear the side of the clubhouse before following.

The sun was higher and hotter. He skipped fourteen and fifteen, the holes farthest from the clubhouse, and on sixteen squatted facing the barn. From the range tee, the man and the boy lofted rainbows.

After Lawson finished eighteen, Mrs. May brought him a glass of ice water and asked how his hand was. Around the picnic table sat eight paunchy men in T-shirts and shorts. Each had a can of Iron City, and one was chewing tobacco. "I know the heat is beastly," Mrs. May said, "but if you would turn off the front nine, these gentlemen could get started. After that you can take a short break."

Lawson wrapped the ice in a paper napkin, put it on top of his head, and pulled his cap on over it. "Hey," one of the men said, "can we get some of that?" A few got up and went into the club-house. "Wait," Mrs. May said, and snatched the empty glass from Lawson and hurried in after them.

Strolling down one, Lawson suddenly felt sorry he had skipped the two holes. Mrs. May was a fair woman (fair and hard like all good people), but she didn't know the least thing about birds. Maybe if she did she wouldn't be the way she was. Not that there was anything wrong with the way she was, being out in the middle of nowhere by herself so long. It wasn't any easier for her, not by a long shot. What she needed was something to take care of besides the course, something to take her mind off her troubles. Pigeons sounded like the answer. He hustled down the fairway, and when he reached the sprinkler didn't linger in the cool jets.

"Wait until he's past the green," Mrs. May told the man on the tee. The other foursome was headed for ten, toting their bags on their shoulders. The old Brunswick carts were in the barn. For a while after Mr. May died, Jonathan came every spring and got them in condition, but he had stopped—when?—it must have been five years now. And Mr. Lawson, for all his work on his car, had not once laid a finger on them.

"What about now?" the man asked.

Mr. Lawson was inching up the slope in front of the sandtraps, two hundred yards away.

"Go ahead," she said.

The man set his beer can down by his back foot, addressed the ball with a loopy half-swing, and sent a line drive screaming across the fifth fairway. "We're playing a mulligan, right, guys?"

Mr. Lawson tromped straight across the green.

The father and son were sitting at the picnic table, and when Mrs. May steamed past, the father said, "I think we were here before they were."

"I'm aware of that," she said, but she had in truth forgotten them, and flustered, not having another answer, she apologized and had them start on sixteen.

She went into the clubhouse and sat behind the counter with a wet washcloth over her eyes. A fan with blue plastic blades turned in its cage. From time to time she lifted a corner of the washcloth and peeked out the door. It would not do to have Mr. Lawson find her like this.

And the city crowd, they would be here any second. The holiday traffic was holding them up, that was all. There had been days, and not so long ago, before the state had built Lake Arthur, when people poured in right after lunch, shot a leisurely eighteen, and stood around the picnic table, sipping gin and tonics. They would ask who won the Firecracker 400, and the men would argue who was the best, Richard Petty, Cale Yarborough, or David Pierson. About dusk, Mr. May would roll out the gas grille and barbecue chicken wings for everyone, and later, when the fireflies and then the bats came out and she put Jonathan to bed, he would light the tiki torches and there would be sparklers and singing. And going to bed, the quiet —

"Miss May, ma'am?"

She whipped off the cloth. Mr. Lawson was standing in the doorway, smiling like an idiot, a V of dirt and sweat darkening his shirt.

"Yes?" she said.

"I'm all done with the sprinkling, the whole thing. Can I take my break now?"

"You can take your lunch, if you remember to make it a short one. We have a lot of work to do."

"I don't see a whole lot of people out there."

"Believe me, there will be. Holidays are always busy."

"It wasn't busy Memorial Day."

"There is a big difference between Memorial Day and July 4th, Mr. Lawson. Everyone celebrates July 4th. Have you once in your life seen people setting off fireworks on Memorial Day?"

"No, ma'am."

"I didn't think so. Now after lunch I want you to paint the signs

on the range. You should be able to see the numbers, but if you
have any trouble, come and ask me. Now go."

Lawson went back to the barn and changed his shirt. He took
a half-gallon of milk from a listing Coca-Cola machine, poured
himself a cup, and added a drop of brandy. On Wednesday Mr.
Bottsie had brought him some olive loaf, but the bread from two
Wednesdays ago had green spots, and the more he cut away with
his pocketknife, the nastier it got. He tossed the bread into the
lower loft. He got into the GTO, set his cap on the red leather
dash, revved the engine, and turned on the air-conditioning. He
laid his head against the headrest and let the glycol-chilled air dry
his neck.

He did not mind Mrs. May talking to him like that. Some
people had funny ways of saying thank you. You could never tell
what people were like by what they said, or even what they did.
Like Danny that one time. He was just mad at having to go. They
were arguing when there was nothing to argue about; when the
man said go, you went. Danny never meant to say what he said,
they were just arguing. And no matter what he said later, when
they didn't talk and acted like they weren't blood, in the end he
went. In the end there had been something between them that
wouldn't let him not go. Lawson drained his milk and killed the
engine.

He pulled himself up the ladder. The tarp over the roost was
undisturbed, the pigeons quiet. He sat on a hay bale, looking up
through the dim, dusty light at the broken window. The bales in
the upper loft were stacked in rows like steps. The top row was
shy of the window a good ten feet.

On his way up, a rung snapped off in his hand. He fell a quick
distance and landed across two bales, stunned but uninjured. He
pressed a hand to the small of his back, waggled his arms and legs
to make sure. Determined, he hugged the ladder, testing each
rung as he went.

The twine on the bales cut into his palms. The hay was rotten

---

and sweet-smelling, and he could not lift it. Thinking of Mrs. May, he climbed down, found a can of white and a can of black latex and two crusty brushes and walked around the barn to the range.

If there was anything worse for arthritis than painting, Lawson didn't know what it was; on the other hand, he was close enough to the barn to keep an eye on the window and far enough away to see the whole sky. He worked sideways, slapping the white on without looking. Flitting swallows made his heart stop and tingle. Grasshoppers sprang in the timothy, distracting him, one falling in the open can.

The signs were taking too long. By the third, his arms were white and sticky and beginning to itch. The sun was directly overhead, there were two signs to go, and he hadn't even started the numbers. He pried the black open, mixed it with a dead branch and began painting the first sign, the 100. Thick and fresh, the white coat hid the originals. His new 1 came out streaked and gray near the bottom. "Mr. Lawson," he said, imitating her, "that is the piss-poorest paint job I've seen in my entire life."

By the time he finished the white, the first sign was tacky. He remixed the black and went over the 1. It took.

As he was adding the first 0, a rabbit burst from a tuft beside him and scampered across the meadow, zigzagging, its ears pinned back. Lawson shielded his eyes. The hawk was wheeling high over the woods, flapping once then gliding, drifting in a long, slow arc. The rabbit splashed through the creek and up the bank, slipped under a strand of barbed wire, and bounded into the woods. As if shot, the hawk dove into the trees. Lawson dropped his brush in the can and ran for the barn.

He came back with the BB gun and waited for the hawk, aiming just above the treetops, steadying the barrel on the sign. After a long five minutes, he lowered the gun, leaned it against the back of the sign, and, crouching so the hawk wouldn't see him, peeking over the top every so often, painted two more 0's.

Checking on him from the clubhouse window, Mrs. May saw him paint the extra 0 and threw her washcloth on the floor. "What is his problem?" she yelled over the Firecracker 400, which she was watching on her portable. She stepped outside and made sure no one was teeing off or putting on the front nine, went back in, and said into the mike: "Mr. Lawson." He turned toward the clubhouse and waved, a brush in his hand. "One hundred, Mr. Lawson, not one thousand, one hundred." He turned to the sign, turned back, and waved.

"The man is obviously trying to drive me insane," she said to a baby in a radial tire. When the race came back on, Richard Petty's son Kyle was leading. He looked like his father except his hair wasn't as greasy. She popped another soda and watched until Darrel Waltrip took the lead. Mr. May had always hated Darrel Waltrip. She switched to the Pirate game, but they were beating the Mets too badly, and the only other thing on was golf. She clicked the set off. You didn't watch golf, you played it. Maybe that was the problem, everyone was home watching golf.

Around three the man and his son came in and bought two cans of soda, then sat at the picnic table, changing their spikes and totting up their scores. Mrs. May offered them a wicker bowl of pretzels and asked them how they did.

"So-so," the man said.

"Tell her about your drive on fourteen," the boy said.

"A nice one?"

"I think the ground being hard helped it out a little."

"It was three hundred, easy."

"You notice I still ended up bogeying the thing," the man said.

"Have you tried putting these greens lately? They're like glass."

"They were kinda fast," the boy admitted.

"It's the drought," Mrs. May explained. "We water twice a day, and it just soaks right in. Next time you come it should be in better shape."

"I don't know," the man said, "we only came over because we

couldn't get a tee time at the Lake Club—and we belong there! I swear, they treat the tourists better than their own members."

"We're open all week," Mrs. May said, "except Wednesdays."

"I'll remember that," the man said, and stood up. The boy stood, chugged his soda and folded the scorecard into his back pocket, and they hauled their bags to the station wagon.

"Drive safe now," Mrs. May said, "and come back soon." When the wagon was safely away, throwing up dust, she said, "Lake Club, the nerve."

She scanned the front nine for the foursomes. One was on the seventh green. A fat man in a dark T-shirt too small for him was swinging the pin like a drum major. Another was pitching beer cans to him. "God help me," she said, "this is what I have to put up with." She went into the clubhouse and turned on the Firecracker 400. Darrel Waltrip now had a lap on the field. She checked on Mr. Lawson. He was up to 200. The beer-drinkers were teeing off on eight. She waited until the fat man was into his backswing before calling over the PA: "Mr. Lawson. Very nice."

Lawson waved and kept painting. "See there?" he said, "and you say she doesn't appreciate you."

Though his elbow was beginning to stiffen, he hurried through the fifth sign. He was getting too close to the woods. If the hawk broke, it would be past him before he could get a shot off. Even if he did, would a BB kill it?

A BB could kill a pigeon, he knew that. That was the whole reason for buying Martin Luther King and the others. He had given Danny the gun for Christmas and the next day found two pigeons in the snow behind their building. They were frozen, and he could hardly tell they'd been shot; only a spot of black blood showed on each breast. He brought them inside and showed them to the boy. The boy denied it. "Hold them," he said, "hold them in your hands." The boy shook. "Look at me. What would your mother say if she could see you like this? Would your mother like what she was seeing?" The boy began to sob, and Lawson realized he had gone too far. He snatched the birds from the boy and threw them in the kitchen trash, which only made the boy cry more. He was not meant to be a parent. He never knew what to do. But in this case—and maybe only in this one case in all of their years as father and son—Lawson had come up with the right answer. In his last letter, seven years almost to the day, halfway across the world, Danny had asked about his birthday birds.

But would a BB kill a hawk? Lawson put down his brush and picked up the gun. There were white fingerprints on the stock and the trigger. He remembered a term from his own hitch in the infantry—muzzle velocity. The higher the muzzle velocity, the harder the bullet hit. His elbow burning, he cocked the lever as many times as he could, fighting the rising air pressure. He'd put a BB right through the son of a bitch.

He cut a notch in the top of the 100 yard marker with his pocketknife, fit the barrel in it, and waited. The paint made him dizzy. A film of sweat warmed his hands. He wiped them on his cap, then put the cap on backwards. His pinky began to sting, his elbow throbbed. He flexed his right arm until it went numb.

Could it have gotten past him? There were those few seconds when he was in the barn, getting the gun. Or maybe it left. Maybe it had killed the rabbit and called it a day.

After a while he decided to call Mr. Bottsie. Maybe the old man had forgotten to set Martin Luther King free. Lawson leaned the gun against the sign and walked across the meadow backwards. At the tee he began to run for the clubhouse.

"It's real important," he told Mrs. May, bending his cap in his hands. She must have had one of her headaches because the TV was off. "It won't take a minute, I promise."

"I want those signs done by the end of the day."

"Yes, ma'am."

Mr. Bottsie answered on the third ring, "Bottsie's Pet Store, this here's Bottsie speaking."

"Mr. Bottsie—"

"—closed right now, but if you got something sick you can come down and bang on the door. Anything else, come by during the week nine-to-five or if you're lucky, Saturday. If you want to leave a message, go ahead. I can't promise you anything." A beep beeped.

"Mr. Bottsie, there's a hawk up here. Whatever you do, don't send Martin." He read the phone number off the dial and just before the beep beeped again, added, "This is me, Lawson." He hung up and looked out the window. The sky over the woods was clear and deepening.

"Mr. Lawson," Mrs. May said to his back.

"Huh?" he asked, giving her a blank look. She didn't smell anything, but he was probably half in the bag by now.

"The signs, Mr. Lawson, the signs."

"Oh yeah," he said, and walked out the door.

He had left his baseball cap on the counter. "Idiot," she said. She heard laughter outside. The beer drinkers, all eight of them, were stumbling across the second fairway, headed straight for her. She slid a pencil through the plastic snap band of the cap, carried it outside, and dropped it on the picnic table.

When they leaned their bags against the side of the clubhouse, empty cans clinked. They plopped down at the picnic table. One man laid his head down on his crossed arms, another put on Mr. Lawson's cap. Two others were soaking wet. "Bud OK?" a wide, tanned man in a black mesh jersey asked the rest of the group. He had hairy shoulders. He stood and repeated the order to Mrs. May, swaying.

"I'm afraid all we have is soda," she said.

"You don't have any beer?"

"I'm afraid not."

The man with his head on the table looked up and said, "What do you mean you don't have any beers?" He got up and came around the table, balancing against it with a hand. He was skinny and wore a Steelers T-shirt and red swim trunks and his eyes were almost closed. "No beers? What kind of place are you running here?"

"Joey, take it easy," the hairy man said, taking the skinny man's arm. The others laughed.

The skinny man sloughed his hand off. "Hey, all I want's a beer. I been out here four stinking hours and now I can't even get a beer?"

"She's got pop; have a pop."

"I don't want a goddamn pop."

"You don't have to pitch a fit, for Chrissake."

"Who's pitching a fit?"

"Gee, let me guess. Who usually pitches a fit when he loses?"

The skinny man hit the hairy man in the face, and they fell to the ground, swinging. Mrs. May leapt backwards and clutched the doorframe.

The other men wrestled the two apart and held them facing each other. They both looked surprised. "What the fuck was that for?" the hairy man shouted. He touched his face and looked at his hand. "You coulda broke my nose!"

They glared at each other, then at the men holding them. Gradually the others let go. Still, nobody moved or said anything.

Finally the skinny man said, "You all right?"

"I'll live," the hairy man said. He wiped his teeth on the back of his hand.

"C'mon," someone said, "let's get out of here and get some beers."

"Yeah," the skinny man said, "this place sucks. Whaddya say, John?"

Everyone looked to the hairy man. "OK," he said, "but you're buying, you ugly fuck."

They made them shake, everyone laughed, and shouting and pounding each other on the back, showing each other how the first punch had landed, they shambled to their cars, two big Dodges, slammed the trunks and doors, and roared away in a cloud of dust.

Mrs. May was still clinging to the doorframe. Where was Mr. Lawson? She could have been killed. He was no help at all. She felt her throat and then her pulse. She slumped into the chair behind the counter and pressed her hand to her heart.

When it was quiet again, she called her son.

"Yeah?" he answered. He practically shouted.

"Dear, it's your mother. The most terrible thing just happened. These men came and drank beer and had this awful fight on the patio. There were eight of them, and they—"

"Mom, I can't talk right now. If this is going to be a long story, you'll have to call me tomorrow."

"Are you listening to me? They were drunk. They could have destroyed the place. There was no one to stop them. I can't go on like this by myself, I can't."

There was silence.

"Jonathan, I need someone to help me. Mr. Lawson is not enough. I need you here."

"Mother." He paused. "Mother, you know that's not realistic."

"I don't care if it's realistic. I can't do it anymore, don't you understand, I can't do it. Your father is gone and I'm all by myself. I'm doing the best I can but I don't think I'll be able to much longer. Please, honey, please. Your mother needs your help."

"Calm down," he said, "you're getting hysterical."

"I am not hysterical," she shouted, and feeling tears coming on, rapped her knuckles hard against the counter. "I am not hysterical," she repeated calmly, "I am simply worried about what is going to happen to this place. I know you don't like talking about it, but, Jonathan, we really do have to talk."

"We'll talk, all right? But right now I've got corn boiling over, Alicia's kid is screaming her head off, I'm the only one here, and fifteen people are going to walk through the door any minute."

"I'm your mother."

"I know you are and I love you, but I've got to hang up now. I'll call you tomorrow." The line clicked.

"Jonathan!"

She did not cry. She sat down at the picnic table with a fresh soda and lit a Carlton. The course was empty, a vast brown waste shimmering in the heat. She let the smoke drift from her lips, then blew it away. There would be more people tomorrow. It was still July 4th weekend. It was the drought and the traffic, that was all. She would have Mr. Lawson turn on the sprinklers before supper.

As she turned the corner of the barn, she saw the half-painted 300 sign and swore. She shouted into the barn. He was gone. "That's it," she said, "no more." On her way back to the clubhouse, she spilled her soda on her blouse.

Martin Luther King cleared the treetops edging fourteen. He flapped and rose, then dipped, coasting, his wings held against him. Lawson ran down the eleventh fairway toward him, waving the gun over his head.

"Mr. Lawson!" a voice boomed from the sky. He stopped and looked back. "Mr. Lawson, I want to see you — now!" Her last word echoed. Beyond the range, as if summoned, the hawk lifted out of the woods.

By the time Martin saw it, it was too late. He darted for the front nine, flapping madly, but he was too slow. Lawson held the stock to his cheek, following the hawk, which climbed out of range, high above Martin, stalled — suspended black against the sky, its wingtips like fingers — and dove. The two birds were directly above Lawson. He waited as long as he could, making sure, before firing his one shot.

Mrs. May spotted him kneeling in the rough beside the access road. Swinging her arms, her fists balled, she crossed the parking lot and advanced on him. When she was in range, she screamed at his bent back, "Why are you doing this to me?"

He did not turn to face her.

"You're killing me, that's what you're doing, you are killing me. Why are you doing this to me? Why?"

She walked around him. He held one of his birds to his chest, a big, fat pigeon, squeezing it with both hands like a rosary. His shirt was soaked with blood, and his face shone with tears. His nose was running; his eyes were wide.

"Mr. Lawson," she said, "Mr. Lawson." She touched his shoulder. "Mr. Lawson!"

"My boy," he said, gazing up at the high blue sky, empty now, "my boy, my boy, my boy . . ."

When she realized he was not going to stop, Mrs. May helped him to his feet and led him away to the clubhouse, both hands around his arm, steadying his elbow like a dutiful child.

In the Walled City

Coming down into Logan over the harbor islands, Grey imagined Rachel and the children waiting for him at the gate, and not, like the dots crawling over Fort Warren below, blissfully isolate, far asea on Nantucket. Other years Grey might have wished he were there, lost in mysteries on the porch, or alone in Boston, free to research and write. This year he'd had no choice in the matter. Rachel had not asked if he could come, and for his part, he had jumped at the university's travel grant.

Ah, but Madaket, the dunes at sunset. They had sailed there, drunk too much, left the windows open. The shudder of the gear lowering kept Grey from his vision. The city shimmered off starboard in August haze, the sea ended suddenly in runway, and with a cushioned jolt Grey's summer in Dijon was over.

A bell rang and everybody jammed into the aisle for their overhead luggage. The cool jet above him stopped. He waited for the others to jostle out and stampede down to the baggage carousels, waited for his three old matching brown bags, waited in the hot exhaust for the shuttle to the T stop to wait for the train that would take him, haltingly, underground to Government Center to wait for a C to Brookline. On this succession of platforms Grey did his best not to think, but stood with his bags massed at his feet, catching up on the stations' advertising, graffiti, and resident homeless. He was home, which should have pleased him, yet he felt himself fending off the beginnings of an empty anger, and as he tacked homeward his resentment took in the whole city. He had money for a cab and several times considered it, but on the C, aboveground again on the long, glinting flat of Beacon Street, a few stops short of his own, Grey was rewarded with the vision of a boy—eighteen at most—with white-blonde hair in a muscle shirt cut to show his midriff. Such offhand beauty stirred him, and for an instant the rattling, drab brownstones seemed to brighten, the sidewalk crowd to pick up a step, the sun to mellow.

Rachel and the children would not be home for a good week. He might call Mason. They hadn't talked since June—transatlantic, crackly—and Grey thought, not altogether honestly, that Mason might have forgiven him where Rachel could not, when it was Mason he had betrayed, Mason sweating out the summer in his rat hole of a studio over Davis Square while he and Rachel fled separately. Mason might have taken up with Rob, his Jamaican friend, again. It was all sordid, regrettable, and by his stop Grey had resolved to become again the husband and father his own father (God bless him, keep him) had failed to be. When it was, of course, too late.

He stepped down and the heat closed over him. It was not quite two. The time difference made his own neighborhood seem both comforting and strange, fake, as if the real Grey would show up in a few hours. Mock-Tudors and big stucco blocks perched back from the street, windows black, blank. Everyone was down on the Cape. A few station wagons baked in driveways, a lawn lay browning. Farther on, the crazy mail-lady in her pith helmet muttered over her pushcart. He would have to get the mail turned on, deal with Rachel's bills. God knew what was waiting for him at school. He and Mason no longer wrote: it had been a stray note Rachel found that started everything.

"Who is Mason?" she had asked that evening on the patio.

"Student," Grey said.

"Male."

"Grad."

She put her drink down and plucked a scrap of legal paper from her pocket. "He says he misses your hands. What could that possibly mean?"

He could not come up with a quick, convincing answer because he could see his thumbs on Mason's waist, between them the downy small of Mason's back.

"I was helping him," Grey said.

"Were you?" Rachel said hopefully, then when he hesitated answered, "Tell me, why do I bother asking?" She had dropped the scrap of paper in his lap and taken her drink inside.

The bags weighed on him. Ah, but Mrs. Abplanalp's garden was prospering, brilliant in the sun. It ran around the iron rail of their porch, a dizzy burst of color. Ralph, his youngest, had tended it one summer while the Abplanalps had their month at Bar Harbor, lugging Rachel's sloshing watering can across the lawn at dusk, and the thought of such painstaking devotion so miraculously rewarded buoyed Grey. He himself was watching a house — if it had once been his own — and perhaps if he tended it diligently he would be welcomed again. The last few weeks of spring semester he had slept on the couch in his office. They had been through it before, in the past had fought to unsatisfying draws whose terms acknowledged his desire and her distaste. Back then, Rachel would eventually relent. So far this time, she'd shown no sign. Her idea was that they should part amicably. The children were old enough, though there was no need for them to know why. He had not thought her so harsh, so impractical. They still had a joint account. He would pay the bills, happy to take care of them. Fine, she'd said, just don't expect anything from me.

The house hadn't burned down. Rachel had probably gotten Sigi Hansen next door to water the plants. It looked like one of the twins had cut the grass. Grey had to put his bags down on the porch to find his keys, and kneeling on the patterned tiles he had hosed down summer evenings for twenty years, wondered where he would go.

The air was musty, the blinds drawn against the sun. He locked the door behind him and went to the fridge, hoping for something cold, but found only some cans of papaya nectar Melanie had recently discovered. He got the scotch out of the pantry and poured himself some over an ice cube, then sat on the couch in the curtained living room and drank, from time to time closing his eyes.

When he had stopped moving, he went back into the kitchen and called the house at Madaket.

"Grey's," Melanie answered. She sounded funny, squeaky.

"Melanie?"

"No. Mr. Grey?"

"Who is this?"

"Lisa." She would be Ralph's or Mark's latest from school; he could not see a face.

"Lisa, is Mrs. Grey around?"

"Everyone's at the beach. I've got a cold."

"I'm sorry."

"Do you have a message?"

"Yes," Grey said, "please tell everyone I arrived safely."

"Should I have Mrs. Grey call you?"

"If she wants to," he said. "It's nothing urgent."

He had to go through the pictures he'd taken in Beaune, put some notes together before the semester started. He had work enough.

He took the plants out of the sink and put them back where they belonged. He called the post office; they said he'd have to come down and sign for their mail. He ate some peanut butter on crackers, drank some more scotch, and found the keys to the squareback. It was Rachel's originally; Mark had driven it hard in high school. It was good for around town, or in winter. A dayglo rubber wolfman swung from the mirror. No one would recognize him, and this pleased Grey. He fashioned a costume of old tennis shorts and a paint-spotted Izod shirt, in the squareback found a dated pair of Mark's shades.

The post office gave him a shopping bag full, most of it junk. At school he snuck up on the mail room, taking a back staircase. The door connecting it with the graduate office was open for circulation. Inside he could see Peggy at her word processor, and while he was tempted to say hello, he kept to the wall of mailboxes. His was crammed, a few envelopes accordioned. Clutching the mess to his chest, he scanned the hallway, then darted across, and quickstepped down the stairs.

Back home, he dumped the pile on the couch and pawed through it, sipping. Nothing from Mason, but a photocopied note said in the anonymous, heartfelt language of departmental missives that Rolandsen had died in Cologne. It gave no explanation, only the when and where of the memorial service. The date was the day after tomorrow.

Grey slumped back into the couch and bit a cracker in half. Rollie, Jesus. He had known the younger man, if he had not been his friend. Politics were involved, the raw obstacles of position and reputation, and horrified, Grey found himself thinking that if things fell the way they should, he would move up and take the empty Marsden chair.

But how young Rolandsen was, late forties, only beginning to be recognized for his early book on the troubadours, when he was far beyond that. He'd been working up a book on the Klafeld heretics; he was in Cologne to go over the original manuscripts. Probably a heart attack the way he ate. Peggy hadn't thought the two close enough to call him in Beaune. And the sick thought came to Grey that while he was flying back coach, nibbling dry corned-beef sandwiches, Rolandsen was below with the cold baggage.

Grey tried Mason but the number was no longer in service. Like Rachel, Mason wasn't good with bills; he'd never had to be. Besides youth's invulnerable cynicism and hope, Mason had a streak of helplessness or ineptitude that gave Grey fits. He was not good with money or at choosing friends, and when Grey admitted worrying about him, Mason, like a child, would either go quiet or laugh it off. "Can't we just enjoy ourselves?" he'd say, in essence saying they weren't going to last (the ashtray cold on his chest, clock in the kitchenette telling him he should get dressed for class), and though Grey knew they could not, some romantic ideal from his youth kept him wishing. How many had he lost, and yet he was always shocked, for weeks a wreck. He clung to his men the same way he clung to Rachel and his family—the lost, sunlit excursions to Crane's Beach or Lake Winnepesaukee, Rachel asleep on the chaise on the back porch, the waving shadow of the maple picking out bright flecks of skin, lip, lash. His two loves seemed equal—right, somehow fated—though when he was with his family for more than a few days he was certain he was paying for a decision made long ago by someone not himself, and in his lover's arms saw Melanie dressed for church.

Grey drove over to Davis Square. Mason's name was still on the same door of the bashed brass mailbox. Grey rang the buzzer, looking up the stairs at the second floor, the weak, naked bulb, then gave up and stood in the ratty vestibule, feeling old and so heavy he thought he would never make it back to the car. He did not pull out of the space, for a time sat in the heat with his keys in his lap. A car pulled up and honked, hoping Grey would leave. Grey looked in the mirror. The wolfman hung from its chain, turning.

"Keep your pants on," Grey said.

He took the phone off the hook, poured himself a coffee cup of scotch and took it to bed.

He worked most of the next morning in the dining room, numbering and labeling his pictures. He had spent the last two months in the walled city of Beaune, in the Hôtel-Dieu, a great medieval bastion, photographing Van der Weyden's *Last Judgment*. A polyptych of death, damnation, and resurrection, it was often cited as the model for Brueghel's *Triumph of Death*. God loomed huge and backlit over a mountain of corpses with crossed arms and closed eyes. Below, sinners tore at themselves, burned broken on wheels, drowned in tides of blood. The Hôtel-Dieu had been a hospital during the plague. The mural covered one monstrous limestone wall of what had been the poor ward. Grey imagined the patients lying helpless under such vivid agonies, face to face with their own ends. The French now ran it as a tourist attraction. They had installed an ingenious, mechanized magnifying glass which inched over the painting's surface like the pointer on a Ouija board, picking out the bugged eyes and clenched teeth of the d...nned. When he had arrived in Dijon, Grey had a book on the cautionary in medieval art in mind, but as the summer wore on he found the *Last Judgment* depressing, obscene, and now he only felt compelled to publish the damn thing to get it out of his system. But he needed something to work on now, some distraction. He fit together the *Last Judgment* on the dining room table like a rainy day puzzle for the children, the pieces big, colors bright, then paced around it taking notes.

He and Mason never had mornings. Grey dreamed of him making coffee naked, or surprising him in the shower. He could see if Rachel had been jealous, the way he had been when they were younger and she came back late some afternoons from tennis, beaming, serving up feeble excuses. They were supposed to be over that, she said, tearful, when she meant she was disgusted, that he was a monster. Mason never made him feel that way, it was only when he was alone.

Over a lunch of tuna fish, he called the department office. It was a heart attack, Peggy confirmed.

"Want to hear the weird thing?" she said. "He was in the rare book room when it happened. With the book."

"With the door locked from the inside, no doubt."

"Better," she said, "he wasn't the first person who died reading that book."

"Don't joke," he said.

"It sucks, doesn't it?" she said. "Poor Rollie."

Like most of his colleagues, Grey did not frequent department functions, and he certainly did not feel like a funeral now. Peggy said she wouldn't be able to make it, though she gave him no hard excuse. He did not want to say it was inconvenient (it was not) or that he had never actually liked Rolandsen. He said he didn't know, he doubted it.

He was not quite drunk when Rachel called — it was hard to judge, not having talked with anyone all evening.

"The weather's been wonderful," she said. "Did you get around to any of the vineyards?"

"No time," he said. "The house is fine. I'm fine."

"Lisa said."

"She's Mark's friend."

"Good guess. She's new. Very nice."

"I got a note at school that said Rollie Rolandsen died a few days ago in Cologne."

"I'm sorry, I don't remember him. Was he a friend?"

"He was about our age."

"Single, is that right, a big man?"

"He was fat. He wasn't much of a social type. He came to the house maybe twice."

"I don't know what to say."

"We were never friends but he was a good man."

"Unlike some in your department."

"Yes," Grey said. "I guess he was more like me, kind of harmless."

"How are my plants?" she asked. "We're thinking of staying another week. Will you be there when we get back?"

"Am I allowed?"

"We've been through this," she said, as if exhausted by the question.

Grey stood at the sink, looking out the window into the dark backyard. "Tell me what you want me to do."

"I don't care," she said. "Make up your own mind."

"I miss you."

"We'll see how the weather holds up."

The squareback rattled all the way to Davis Square. He chewed gum and smoked, hoping they would help if the cops stopped him. It was sweltering, and the sidewalks were crowded, the stairs to Mason's building a gantlet of young West Indian men drinking beer and laughing with what seemed to Grey calculated menace. Rob was not among them, but the first purred words in patois were enough to temper Grey's hopes.

He buzzed and waited, buzzed again and was ready to go when a figure appeared at the top of the stairs. The bulb behind the man made it hard to see, but halfway down Grey recognized Mason, looking fit in jeans and a tank top, his feet bare. He'd been out in the sun; his hair held an auburn tint and his arms were dark. He gave Grey a sour smile, opened the door but held on to the frame.

"I tried to call."

"I don't need a lecture."

"If Rob's here," Grey offered.

"No one's here." He stood blocking the door. Grey could not help but remember him differently, more boyish, but could find no sign in his face.

"I don't know why I came."

"I'm sorry," Mason said, as if he couldn't help him.

"Are you all right?"

"I'm doing fine."

"How's your money?"

"It's fine," Mason said.

Above, at the top of the stairs, a figure asked, "Everything cool, Mace?"

"Yeah," Mason called, then said to Grey, "I'll see you at school."

"Be careful."

"I'll see you," Mason said.

The men on the steps roared when Grey came out, their laughter following him down the street.

He could not look at the *Last Judgment,* the lost slit like fish. The rain held off until midnight and didn't cool anything down.

Grey sat on the patio, sipping and listening, thinking of the vege-table garden they used to plant, the inflatable pool with the blue bottom the children lounged in, lunch under the maple. That, he thought, was the mystery, how all of that had vanished while the house stayed the same.

The service was in the morning at a funeral home over in Cam-bridge. It was humid and overcast, threatening, and Grey made sure he was late. He parked the squareback on a side street off Mass Ave. He had on a linen suit he used to wear Sundays when the children were younger. It was not as light as he remembered. The funeral home was air-conditioned, heavily carpeted, and dark. There were several viewing rooms, and following a stand-ing menu board he mistakenly entered the first one, empty save a casket. He backtracked to the main hall where a man in a beau-tiful charcoal suit said yes, that was the Rolandsen room.

"Is the family here?" Grey asked.

"I do not believe Mr. Rolandsen has any family in the area." He said it with such composure and — Grey liked to think — com-passion, that Grey accepted it as normal, even right. A man his age, unmarried. This time of year the city was empty; it was un-fortunate, nothing more.

The coffin was closed. Grey took a seat halfway back among the padded folding chairs and waited. He was only a few blocks from Davis Square. Mason would just be waking up, ready for a full day in the stacks of the Widener.

The director walked up the aisle to Grey and said the proces-sion would begin momentarily. If he would bring his car around?

He followed the hearse, checking in the mirror for latecomers, but none showed. He wished he had air-conditioning. The funeral home supplied the priest and the pallbearers, leaving Grey with nothing to do but stand by the open hole, leafing through the complimentary program. The service went on for pages. The heat and low clouds brought out the smell of turned earth. He expected some friend or lover to rush over the shadowed grass, bearing flowers. He wanted it all to mean something to somebody. A sudden panic welled over him, and he fought it by gazing far over the neat rows of stones.

It was a nice cemetery, clean, well-tended, and desperately Grey thought that Rolandsen would appreciate his coming. Across a pond a backhoe tore at the grass. One of the pallbearers pushed the button and the mechanized lift lowered the box; the priest let fall the handful. Grey thought of Rolandsen inside, hearing it hit; the calm expression of the dead. He had studied hell all summer, but only now did the real threat of the *Last Judgment* hit him. Van der Weyden had taken his subjects not from life but from the Hôtel-Dieu's newly dead, so that those patients still living watched the painter — sometimes the same day — recreate their neighbors' faces. For the first time since his father's funeral, Grey said a prayer. He thanked the director, picked his way through the stones, got in the squareback, and drove.

The sky was blazing, the sidewalks empty. He passed a T with a few dark heads in the tinted windows but no cars, no one walking. Was it a holiday, or was he the only one left in the city?

The Abplanalps had hired landscapers; their stake truck sat in the driveway, rakes and shovels fitted into the sides like weapons at the ready. An older man knelt by the flower bed with a pair of shears, another stood on a short ladder, shaping the hedge. A boy a little younger than Ralph was pushing a deafening gas mower over the yard. He had his shirt off, and at the small of his back his shorts were dark with sweat. He saluted Grey as he passed.

Inside, Grey drew the curtains so he wouldn't have to see them. He took apart the *Last Judgment,* wrapping a rubber band around the stack of pictures. He closed all the windows and put the plants in the sink. He took the checkbook and an old pair of tennis shorts, left a note in the Hansens' mailbox. The squareback shuddered when it hit fifty, the wolfman shimmered. He stopped at a Store24 outside Quincy for a pair of sunglasses and a paperback murder which tempted him but which he did not touch, instead sleeping, arms crossed over his chest, as the Hyannis boat rocked through the falling dark.

Calling

The school bus brakes by the mailbox, a shift of dust and leaves passing as it stops, and out of the door steps Walter, the driver. Far up the double rutted drive, the house has lost its height. Walter notices the flag of the mailbox and reaches in for the sheaf of envelopes. Waste grasses flank the sides of the drive, whipping the wind as he trudges toward the remains of the house. The land beyond the rise comes into view, tan gone gray, stubbled harvest fields, reaper tracks visible. Halfway, he turns to make sure the children haven't left the bus. He can't see their faces, only shapes in the split windows. The grasses twitch and whistle, wave to throw off their seed.

He begins to run, work boots gouging dark moons in the dirt, and as he sprints, shocked at his own speed, as he nears, pumping, he sees there is nothing to run to. Fire has reduced the house to a pile of beams. Yet he does not stop until he reaches the border of seared, blackened grass. In the wreckage sit a stove and refrigerator, their paint bubbled. Walter looks back down the drive to the bus, a matchbox against the woods.

The barn is intact, as are all the other out-buildings. Before he reaches the barn the stink hits him. Holding his breath, he knocks, hoping to rouse a lowing, ear to the gnat-specked door. Then he must run to exhale.

Walking back, Walter sees the children's faces take on eyes, smiles. They are laughing — hurry, sit down, here he comes — and when he climbs on and closes the door, giggles escape. He pops the glove compartment and stuffs the mail between greasy maps.

Three cheers for the bus driver
The bus driver, the bus driver
Three-ee chee-eers for the bus driver
Who's with us today
God bless him — he needs it!
God bless him — he needs it!
Three-ee chee-eers for the bus driver who's with us today

When the children are all off, he pulls across a brace of handicapped spaces, kills the engine and heads for the principal's office.

At the Luna, Kennadaro's only bar, Jim Ed Steckler is drunk and telling whoever will listen his plans for his next farm. There are others here in worse shape, farms already gone, working shifts at Nabisco in Chickasha or at Harvester up in Carnegie. They listen respectfully, join in damning the seventies land barons, the banks, the presidents who betrayed them, but they know Jim Ed will never farm again, just as they will never farm again. "Hole gets too big, you're shoveling on yourself," they say. They run up tabs a beer at a time, discussing the Sooners and Wildcats, sipping, listening to Jim Ed rip his guts out at the rail.

"You think I'm gonna work one of those corporate bastard's farms, you're fucked in the head. Goddammit, there's still the land, we never given up on it yet and we're not gonna start now." He drops his cigarette and, retrieving it, knocks over a stool with his hip. "Goddamn shit." Marley Simms, his nearest neighbor, also failing, picks up the stool and turns Jim Ed back to the bar, one flannel arm over his shoulders. The others turn back to their beers, muttering. There is no one to fight here, only in Washington or New York. Paper pushers, politicians.

Jim Ed sees himself in the mirror, beheaded by a fence of bottlenecks. His eyes squint through the smoke, bringing his cheeks up, compressing his face. He laughs at the long-jawed man in the Deere cap, trades a beer salute. They wipe their mouths on their sleeves. Marley guides the mug down to the coaster.

Nadine Steckler worries the children into their chores, reminding them several times while they wash up. Jim Junior, waiting in his pajamas for the bathroom, grunts, "Yeah, Ma." To save electricity they heat and light the house with kerosene, and dawn and dusk Nadine wanders through the halls with a hurricane lamp. The children make amateur ghost noises, shadows fly up the staircase. While she knows they are going to lose the farm, Nadine can't imagine being thrown off the land with nothing to their name besides the pickup. But it is true, she thinks, that is exactly what is going to happen.

After the children's breakfast, alone at the sink, she watches the girls go off to their chores, beyond them the fields, and far off, in patches, the Washita bottomlands. She rinses, gazing up into the clear autumn sky, listening to the cyclic rumble of the milkers. Jim opens the barn door, waves and rubs his stomach. She holds up a hand: five minutes.

He is from Oklahoma City, because none of the locals will touch the job. The FDIC has hired him as far away as the Dakotas for the same reason. He stays at the County Line Motel outside of Kennadaro, fearful of the townspeople. Some of his fellow auctioneers look down on him for doing this kind of work, and he himself feels guilty at times, but it is a job. There are few happy auctions, most are bankruptcy or death. Death attracts a better crowd; bankruptcy, more money.

He eats at a steakhouse next to the motel, reviewing a list of merchandise provided by the FDIC. Though he has never worked on a farm, he can estimate how large and successful it is by the lists. He circles the items most likely to draw high bids. Representatives from the large farms will keep the prices reasonable on most of the machinery; the state government will take the land. He looks for possible antiques among the stray pieces of surviving furniture — the effects, they are called. Bureau, children's, ca. 1850, light smoke damage. He finishes his pie and coffee and picks up the check. From the kitchen service window the cook and the waitress watch him read "Have a nice day. Fuck you." He leaves his regular tip.

The auctioneer sleeps in his car in the woods. He has the date, time, and place; he will be there when they need him. The gun he usually keeps in his suitcase is under the driver's seat, butt out, safety off.

The only picture the editor has of Jim Ed Steckler is from the Kennadaro High yearbook, *The Ram*. Beneath the acned, buzz-cut teen runs, "4-H I, II, IV; varsity basketball III, IV; motoring club. Jim looks forward to a career in agricultural engineering. College: Undecided."

Nadine Smithson is in the next year's edition, her blonde hair tightly pulled back, two banana curls like pillars framing her broad face.

Jim Junior is a white head, his body hidden by a driving forward, the bleacher crowd dark, lost beyond the flash. The ball, between the opposing player's fingertips and the rim, commands his attention. His mouth is open, his eyes wide. The editor finds it inappropriate.

Carolyn June Steckler and Marcia Lynn Steckler do not appear in his files. He searches the elementary school homeroom photos, but their faces are too small, and blowing them up would make them grainy.

He settles for *The Ram* shots, doubled. On the front page they are seventeen years old.

Nadine goes into town once a week with Myra Simms. With the telephone shut off, Nadine needs these trips to catch up on gossip. But lately there has been little to say. Both the Simmses' and Stecklers' finances are dwindling, and Nadine and Myra have run out of wishful solutions. Each trip, after a few minutes of speculation, they ride silently, watching the miles of fence snake by. In town they walk the store aisles, pointing to things they like, then leave without buying.

Before the letters from the credit association and the sheriff's office began, Nadine would wait at the front window for the mail jeep. She walked down the drive in her apron, fresh from the heat of making lunch for the girls. There were flyers from the stores in town and coupons from clearinghouses and letters from her mother. On the way back to the house, the coupons and flyers tucked in her apron pocket, she would read her mother's letters out loud. Now, the girls in school, the mail threatening, she sits in the back room, reading library novels, trying to ignore the approaching engine.

Sometimes Jim Ed comes home from town drunk, but she understands. He has been as good a husband as she had hoped for when she was young. On those nights he comes home drunk, she prepares his supper specially and shoos the kids upstairs. After he eats they sit in the back room and talk. They will move, they will both get jobs in town, or in Carnegie or Chickasha. Everything will work out fine, she says. Everything will be all right.

Fridays, Liza Radley's parents drive her to Chickasha to see a psychiatrist. One night, the week after the fire, they found her bed empty, her window open. Mrs. Radley checked the dresser: nothing was missing. Fearing kidnappers, Mr. Radley called the sheriff, tugged his boots on, grabbed his shotgun, and ran to their Bronco, dragging his wife by the hand. They coasted across the fields, fog lights on, shouting her name. In the beams she glided, her confirmation dress trailing, the lace hem muddied. When her mother helped her into the cab, Liza said, "Thank you very much."

She will have to stay at home until her feet heal, but the doctor says there is no permanent damage. The psychiatrist tells her parents it is a normal reaction. The Radleys hope he is right, know he is wrong.

His bobber drifting, cap pulled down over his face, Jim Ed sees a green mosaic through the nylon mesh. He has told Nadine he is posting the back fence with No Hunting signs for the early doe season. Every few minutes he jerks the line, expecting nothing, happy to be here, away from everything. But he is not away; they are going to take the farm, and nothing he can do will stop them. He has thought of it since the first letter arrived, hoped against it, as if wishing will make things better. He and Nadine have skimmed their possible escapes, but have no real plans. In the calm—birds, leaves, grass—Jim Ed imagines the farm, imagines his entire life as it could have been, reminding himself that it is not.

The line digs into his finger, pulling him out of his thoughts. He stands, his cap falling to the ground. The fish yanks to the left, then weakly to the right and dives, dunking the bobber. Jim Ed squats at the edge of the pond and gives him some slack, then reels in. It is a sunfish, spike-finned, rainbow-oiled. Jim Ed tears the barb through the lip and flings the fish high over the pond like a frisbee. It smacks the surface and disappears.

The girls are in the chicken coop, arguing over their two chicks, Timmy and Tony. Carolyn says Timmy is Tony and that Marcia is stealing him. Marcia counters, accusing Carolyn of trying to steal Timmy from her. They make fists and shout at each other. "Damn," Marcia says accidentally, and Carolyn runs for the hatch, pretending she is going to tell Mother. Marcia catches her by the arm and trips her, and they roll on the floor, kicking and punching. Crying, Caroline escapes to the house. Marcia switches the chicks, then runs to the barn and hides in the hayloft. She waits in the heavy, sweet air. She thinks she hears Mother calling her name, far away, like in a dream. Is it Mother? Marcia knows she will have to come down soon. It is almost dark out.

On a stool in the Luna, Marley Simms overhears:

"Heard he's offered a job and turned it down, insurance job."

"Can't blame him. Wasn't born to be any insurance man, no one's born for that."

"Sometimes a person's got to take what he can get."

"And sometimes you've got to take a stand. You can't let yourself be run around by money all the time."

"It's a damn sight better than what he did do. At least you can keep up living on a job, no matter how bad or low-paid. You can get by."

"So they threw him a bone, that's real nice. Must've made him feel real fine. Insurance job my ass."

"Might've saved his life."

"Now don't talk that way about Jim Ed. He's as good as any one of us."

Liza Radley and Jim Junior sprawl in the backseat of his Chevelle, smoking cigarettes. Both wear black concert T-shirts with silkscreened dragons snorting gold spangles. Their bare legs balance on the frontseat headrests. On the dashboard lie the remains of their post-game snack, cold half-eaten burgers and limp fries. Outside, the Washita boils in the dark trees. They lie back and listen, passing a heavy wine bottle, silent, tired, glad.

The glow of her cigarette sheds a faint electric orange over her thighs and down the ridge of her shins. Jim wants to remember it all, wants to believe he is actually here; the girl beside him, the girl he has just made love with, must be in his imagination. He feels the towel under his thighs, the chill fall night, the cold wet-

ness in his pubic hair. He sees her lips and eyes burning with
beads of light, her face sculpted shadows. Drunk, excited, he
promises to remember.

And why tonight? He has asked her before, pleaded, coaxed,
yet always she cried, denied him. They had done everything but.
Why tonight? He knows enough not to ask. He knows he will
never know why.

State troopers separate the auctioneer from the bidders. They
stand, arms folded, occasionally sneaking a look back at the drab
crowd behind them. From his lectern (Marcia's dresser on end,
black ash with greening copper knobs), the auctioneer conducts.
Here and there he recognizes a face, places a concern. He touts
the machinery in a quick, even voice. The locals try to save some
of their buddy's gear but can't compete with the pros from out of
state. It seems fixed, two bids and a sale, two bids and a sale. Each
time he brings his gavel down, the townspeople shout and swear.
A new reaper, twenty-foot McCormick, goes for thirty thousand,
and the troopers' eyes sweep the crowd.

If it were him, the auctioneer thinks, he would not even come.
He would not be in that position. He would hate the auctioneer,
but at the same time understand. It is not the auctioneer who is
taking his farm. The crowd speaks for the dead. They would kill
me, he thinks, they would kill all of us. There will be pushing and
maybe a punch or two thrown, but in another hour he will be on
the road back to Oklahoma City, gunning his rental car to keep
up with the trooper escort.

The pros ignore the effects, which calms the locals. They save
what they can. The auctioneer calls them, finishes and leaves,
safely. Miles out of Kennadaro, he realizes he has forgotten Marcia's dresser.

Nadine chats with the other shoppers more than she shops.
Without the girls to look after, she rolls up one aisle and down

the next, reading the labels of goods she has never had time to examine. Kippers, oyster sauce, guava jelly. Three-fifty-nine for such a little can! She compares the store's produce and meat with their own, shakes her head at the wax and fat and preservatives. Her list is small: shampoo, toothpaste (she selects a new toothbrush for Jim Junior, replaces it instantly), toilet paper, marjoram, brown sugar, coffee. Generic products beat coupons.

Waiting for Myra on a bench outside, Nadine watches other wives pushing carts heaped with bags and thinks about assistance, food stamps, welfare. She has always voted against these, but how else will they get along? Somehow, she doesn't know exactly, but they will. It is not their fault, they have worked hard. They are not welfare cases, they are taxpayers. Food stamps.

The sheriff waits until everyone else has left, the reporters, the firemen, the coroner; waits until the coroner's wagon clears the end of the lawn, then pokes through the rubble with his boots trying to find it again. In what had been the back room, he kicks it loose, a melted metal rod, a rifle barrel. Before picking it up, he looks back to the road.

There is a pond down the hill.

The last cow falls softly, steel jugs holding the ring of the shot. Jim Ed Steckler closes the barn door and walks up toward the house. It is a cold night, starless, the moon drifting obscured. He gropes the back door for the handle.

In kerosene softness they sit on the couch, the girls on either side of Nadine, Jim Junior on the end, limp, as if asleep during a late movie. Jim Ed rocks, twisted in the dead convex screen, wrapped in flapping shadows. The rifle leans against the coffee table, throws a black beam up the wall and halfway across the ceiling. Jim Ed reaches down and knocks the lamp over, pushes back and waits for the light.

Winter Haven

My father calls about the grass. It's December, I'm trying to sell our place, and we've got a squatter jumping house to house down the beach, building fires on the marble floors.

"You said once a week," my father says, "it's more like once a month."

It's long distance — peak hours — and I pay no matter who calls. That's all going to change once Eileen gets the papers together. The market's depressed, and I'm eating Corn Flakes a lot.

"Look," I tell him, "I'll give him a call, all right?"

"I don't want to be a pain in the ass about it."

"You are being," I say, to let him know he isn't.

"So when are you coming down?"

"Christmas."

"When Christmas?"

"Things are crazy up here," I say, and end up telling him about Eileen.

"That's a shame," he says. "I bet you feel different now, don't you?"

"It's a collarbone."

"That's not the point," he says.

"All that's over," I say, "and I'm not going to talk about it."

He shuts up to make me feel bad.

"I'll call the guy," I say.

I'm living in the guest room off the kitchen so Sandy the realtor can show the house looking nice. The furniture's here; Eileen only took the kids. I have the drapes open and the shades up, the rug's just been shampooed. I've taken down all the crosses except Dan's over my bed. I keep at the dishes, the counters. It's with the multiple listing; when I get off swing shift I find cards by the sink. I'll leave a few rounds on the dresser to give them a thrill.

"He's a detective," Sandy or Barb or Gerry will say. It sounds better than a plain cop, like the pay was really different.

The buyers'll give Dan's Jesus the eye, and depending on the sell, Sandy will or won't tell the story. I wonder what they think I'm going to do. I wonder if they have any suggestions.

Swing isn't as bad as graveyard. Everything's open, and you don't have to change the way you sleep. The day is basically the same, the meals and everything, you just call dinner lunch. You're never late for work.

I don't like to be in the house days. I'll drive down to the ocean and read the Psalms, which sometimes works. I have the department Blazer while I'm on the squatter. The waves come up the sand until they're under me.

> *O Lord my God, in thee do I take refuge;*
> *save me from all my pursuers, and deliver me,*
> *lest like a lion they rend me,*
> *dragging me away, with none to rescue.*

My father hates Winter Haven, the people always out. He says he wants to come back north now that my mother is gone. He doesn't have any friends in Florida, he misses the winter. When the spray is blowing and the gulls hover and the wind herds the trash barrels, I can see the attraction, but the old place is gone, and his friends are dead. But you can't tell him that.

"Any luck?" I ask Sandy.

"Things will pick up with the weather, it's just a buyer's market right now. One problem is people with children don't like breaking up the school year, and that's I think who we're looking for, a family with children. Unfortunately you know what the economy is like around here, I think that's keeping the market slowed down, but things will pick up I'm sure come March, it's just a slow time of year normally."

Eileen's face is coming along but she has to wear a sling, and I have a hard time stopping my sympathy. Once on a bust I fell into a boat and broke my hand. I hated her cutting my food; no matter what it was, halfway through it was cold.

"You want pizza five times a week?" she said. "You want hot dogs and hamburgers like a little kid?"

Our squatter dumps in the toilets but they're capped for the winter. It hits you a foot in the door, that and the smoke. He snips the alarms, even the big ADT systems, that's why Jimby thinks it's a pro. Jimby's from the city; to him if you can fix a car you're a genius. When I was a kid we used to do the same thing, that's why I'm swing and Jimby's days. Jimby comes in, there's an address on his desk, something-something Dune road, and by the time I get in it's pictures. A dried dump, charred ends of driftwood by a grand piano. I put on my duck gear and roam the dunes around the empty houses. Baymen say the sea talks if you listen, but I'm safe. God isn't like a star that can go out.

The grass guy says he's been there. "914 Clarendon," he says, "I got it right in front of me."

"What's the date?"

"Says Thursday."

"This Thursday."

"The Thursday just was."

"What about this Thursday?"

"It doesn't grow that fast."

"Then what, will you tell me, am I paying forty dollars a month for?"

"I'll go and do it again myself if you want."

"Please," I say.

I don't like talking on the phone with the kids. I don't know what she's said to them. "Your old man's not so bad," I say sometimes, but they don't bite. Jay wouldn't trust me even if things were normal; twelve's an ugly age. I expected some help from Dan, but he's gone quiet. It's a bad sign, I say to her, but she thinks I'm getting on her about the whole thing. "Maybe I should move back in," she says. "Sure. Give me a minute to pack everything up, OK?"

She doesn't bother to argue anymore. She'll hear it's me and hang up. She thinks the restraining order takes care of everything. Her sister's the one I feel bad for. Jenny's always liked me. "She's very confused right now," Jenny'll tell me outside. We both know it's not true but it makes leaving easier, and she watches me walk away from the porch like I'll be coming back.

I've got the profit figured at sixteen thousand, clear. When the car commercials come on, I think about walking into the dealer and dropping an envelope on the desk and just pointing to the one I want. Not that we're going to get close to what we're asking.

I like to four-wheel at night, rolling slow over the dunes. The surfcasters' fires hop out of the darkness, then black. A camper forms, battened down for the night. I've got the kids' mattresses in back, beef jerky on the dash, my basic ordnance. It's not going to be easy to go back to the Caprice. I send the spotlight out over the water; even at night, it is still coming.

> *O Lord my God, if I have done this,*
> *if there is wrong in my hands,*
> *if I have requited my friend with evil*
> *or plundered my enemy without cause,*
> *let the enemy pursue me and overtake me,*
> *and let him trample my life to the ground,*
> *and lay my soul in the dust.*

I don't have trouble sleeping, I just forget a lot lately. Jimby leaves me an empty pack of Salems, half-burnt, a blackened matchbook with JFK's face, and a pair of dead AA batteries. He has on a note card, "Menthol Crack Walkman?" I go down to the property room and get something to keep me going. I'm supposed to drop by the rest area past exit 66 and shine my light into the bushes, but when I get there I open the window and listen to the rustle of the men. When is love not evil?

The lights are on at Jenny's, the curtains drawn. Jay's bike lies on its side on the front lawn. I eat a stick of beef jerky and watch the shadows cross and recross the living room window.

Sandy calls and wakes me up to tell me we have a buyer. I'm in last night's camo and still going. My eyes are like tinfoil, my gums sweat. The offer is eighty-seven-five.

"That's not even close," I say.

"No one is getting list value out here right now. If I were in your position I'd think about a serious counteroffer."

"Things are going to pick up in a few months in the spring, is that right?"

"I can't predict the market," she says. "They're a good risk for a mortgage."

"One-oh-two."

"I don't think they'll like that."

My pump leans in the corner. Dan's Jesus bleeds down over me.

"Oh well," I say.

Jimby comments on my beard. "You're really getting into the part," he says, pointing at my hunting vest, my orange hat. They're my own clothes.

"So," I say, "how close are you?"

"Don't get wise," he says, "how're you holding up?"

"Aces, Jimby. I'm living the life."

Jenny's husband, Howie, bowls Tuesdays and Thursdays in Hampton Bays. He rolls three strings then yuks it up in the bar, two pitchers max. The season is on a chart on the wall; it's not half over. This cheap crank makes me see funny, but it looks like Howie's the team's anchorman. Good for fucking you, Howie.

"Jay," I say.

"We're not supposed to talk to you," he says, and hangs up.

The men groan in the bushes. I go down to the beach and shine my fog lights into the houses, go home and sleep till noon. Sin is no enemy.

I've got to remember to eat more often, and then when I try

to have cereal the milk is bad. I feed the cards into the disposal, pour the clotted milk in, and grind it all. The buyers are fuckheads.

"The grass," my father says, "no one came about it."

"I will take care of it," I say, "I swear if I have to come down there myself and cut it."

"I'm the only one here," he says. "You don't know what it's like."

"Do you want me to come down?"

"What about Eileen and the kids?"

"They're gone."

"That's a shame," he says. "Now don't worry about this thing with the grass. I know you've got problems."

"I'm absolutely fine," I say, "I'm just worried about you."

"Don't," he says, "I won't be in your hair much longer."

The guy at the grass place says there was nothing to cut but he ran the mower over it anyway. He gives me the address again. "Does your father have a problem with his memory maybe?"

"How much do I owe you total?" I say, "because I am sick of this bullshit."

Thursday our squatter's camped out at the Flamingo Club in the empty swimming pool and risks a fire because of the windchill. Jimby's coming back from a long lunch at the Crow's Nest and practically trips over the smoke. A local kid, what did I say? I get a change of shift day which takes me through the weekend, then Monday it's back to shaving.

I get down to the beach before sunset. The wind is up, the surf bucking. A few men in waders are letting fly. I've got the heater blasting, a cold six on the seat, my box of Flakes. I can't remember if I took the two I usually take around now, and take four to make sure. The sea never gets tired, never gives up.

O let the evil of the wicked come to an end,
but establish thou the righteous.

I fill up at a Hess and buy two of their Christmas tankers and drive over to Jenny's. They have a tree and presents under it, angels with pipe cleaner wings. Howie's into his second game. Either none of us or all of us are forgiven.

Jenny doesn't understand what I'm doing there. I hand her the tankers through the crack in the door and show her the gun.

"Ron," she says, but won't stop looking at it. I open the door and she steps back.

"Who is it?" Eileen calls from upstairs.

"It's me," I say.

She comes to the top of the stairs. "Jen, are you all right?"

"She's fine," I say.

"What do you want?" Eileen says.

"I wanted to say good-bye. I'm going to Florida. I brought these for the kids." I point to the tankers.

"Good-bye then," Eileen says.

"Good-bye," I say, and shoot her through the sling. She falls back instead of down the stairs so I can just see her feet, flopping. I figure the one's good enough.

I steer clear of the rest areas, sleep in the campgrounds. In the Carolinas everyone's friendly and has extra razors. Driving, I imagine a cop pulling me over, looking in my side while I pretend to get my registration. He'll figure I'm a regular guy and ask, "What's the lawnmower for?" and I'll say, "To cut grass with," and then who knows what will happen.

Finding Amy

Annie Marchand finds the mitten at the foot of the drive. Amy has a runny nose and shouldn't be out too long. Annie is sick herself, the flu has her couch-bound, a glass of flat ginger ale by her head. This is no time for games. She calls both ways, arms crossed, holding her nightgown to her chest. She has long johns on and her boyfriend's boots, unlaced. The red flag is up, in the box a Fay's circular with garden things on the front. She calls and calls.

They have been making love all night, off and on, glazing the sheets, filling the room with smoke. Brock likes her on top; Glenn never waited for her to decide. It is cool above the covers. She leans back, her hands finding a place to land outside his legs. Brock's palms run up her front. In the next room Amy cries out in her sleep, and Annie stops. "Do you want to go see?" he says, but Annie waits, head turned sideways, not breathing. Then grinds on him, thinking—if only for him, for him waiting for her answer—that she needs the divorce.

It is dark inside to save on the electric. Plastic covers the windows; the winter glow makes the carpet look ratty. She turns down "The Guiding Light" and calls through the house. Buster, under the TV tray, hoping for graham cracker crumbs, rises and trots after her. The lunch dishes wait by the sink, Amy's plate with its bear hanging onto a rising bunch of balloons, an elbow straw nodding out of the matching cup. The shower curtain draws back on rubber flowers. She gets a rug burn looking under their bed, finds Barbie's blouse, and with it in one hand and the mitten in the other, heads for the front door, repeating her name.

Glenn has to drive over there if he wants to talk to her. She hangs up on him if he calls. He is living with Rafe, an old high school buddy from work, out past the middle school. Both of Rafe's parents are dead, as are Glenn's. The furniture is deep oak, the rugs frayed bare. They talk, nodding drunk, late at night when they know they have to get up for work, of how Amy is the only thing Glenn has ever done right in his life. Rafe is sterile. He holds Glenn and sobs, trying to explain himself. "You've got Amy, man, no matter what happens, you've got her, man."

"Come on, man," Glenn says, "don't start this shit again."

"You're right," Rafe says, sniffling, trying to laugh. "You know I can't help it."

Out by the water tower the road ends at a striped guardrail. The fields swell into distance, cut by iced-over creeks lined with leaning weed trees. Power lines dip away, spidery towers stride off into fog. The dead stalks rustle. It has begun to snow.

May, Annie's mother, worries that Brock is taking advantage of Annie. Glenn has only been gone a few months, and supposedly the two were friends. Not that she has any sympathy for Glenn, leaving her daughter a four year old and no way to support herself. How she is getting the money May doesn't know, certainly not from what she makes waitressing weekends at the country club. Everytime she asks Annie, they end up fighting. She has always felt — though never said, or only to Martin, softened — that Annie is not a very smart person, that she doesn't look ahead and then is surprised when things go wrong. Dennis, their older boy, did a stint in the Marines, and Raymond worked his way through the community college. Annie still seems to be back in high school, working part time, picking which boy she will give herself to, as if her acts have no consequences. She is their youngest, and according to everything May has heard, she should be clinging to her for dear life. May just wishes she would settle down or, if that will never happen (and she fears this, her only girl), move away where she won't have to see it. But she would miss Amy terribly.

Annie has seen a man in a blue car under the water tower a few times in the last month. Brock asked his cousin the cop; no one seems to know him. They figured he was harmless, an old guy sitting there by himself. Now she sees him watching their house, maybe her and Amy building a snow fort, sees behind his raised newspaper his hand, working.

Brock gets stoned at lunch in the far end of the parking lot with Alicia from payroll. She is heavy and blonde and fun and from Ford City. She loves Neil Young.

"I'm living with Kenny," she says, "but when it's permanent I'll feel it, you know?"

"And it's not right now."

"Kenny? Are you kidding? We grew up together."

"Same with me and Annie." The heater cranks, a leaf stuck in the fan. Smoke leaks out the window. She likes him, he knows, she lets him look into her eyes. He has been trying to figure out why he thinks he is in love with her. Maybe he is not as in love with Annie anymore. He does not want to hurt Annie, but he thinks Alicia may be expecting something more than friendship, and he would not be unwilling.

"The Needle and the Damage Done" takes him inside the dash, into some lost summer night, a dark back road. The roach falls apart. Alicia has gum and gives him a stick. Behind them a few cars cruise for a spot; the front office people are getting back from

the Forbidden City, Rick's Cafe, HoJo's. Alicia reaches over the
stick to put her Visine back in the glove compartment, and they
kiss, the gum sweet between their tongues.

"Ay-meee!" Annie calls, "Ay-meee!" and runs around the house
clumsily, the boots flopping. Buster paces the edge of the woods.
Frozen footprints scamper under the clothes carousel. The rab-
bits are in the porch for the winter, Buster's house odorless in the
cold. She stands with her arms limp, breathing steam. The trees
are bare, a few birds gliding above the tangle, lighting and calling. The paths down in back run clear around the pond and up
to the interstate. She can hear the trucks far off, the whine of their
chains.

Karleen is going to forgive Annie, but only after she's made her
suffer, not a little either. Things were not completely over between
her and Brock, everybody knew that. Maybe he was not her true
love (the way they used to talk about love in school) but she'd given
him three years, more than she had with anyone else. She moved
out of her mother's house into the apartment above McCrory's
for him. She and Annie had talked and talked then, about marriage and being faithful and about love. When she broke up with
Brock, she and Annie sat out on the fire escape, watching the
PBA team scrimmage in the churchyard, the ball making the
chain net ring. Karleen cried, and Annie gave her swigs of pep-
permint schnapps from her flask and made her laugh. It hadn't
been two months when she saw his Grand National in the VFW
lot. She and some of her girlfriends were going stag, for laughs.
She wondered who the hard-up bitch was. She thought it would
be funny.

The porch is jammed with summer junk. She runs around the
last side of the house, fingers cold now, looks up and down the
road, the ditches, calling, then sprints inside. Putting on her own
boots, she calls her nearest neighbor Melvina and explains the

---

situation. It calms her. Melvina has the car today because it is Thursday, and Thursday her mother visits her friends at Overlook. She will bring her mother along, and they can check the fields and woods, and then if they haven't found her, drive around looking. Annie does not have a better plan. She runs through the house with her coat on, calling — throwing Barbie's blouse into the sink — then runs outside.

The car stalls on Melvina.

"Diesel has to warm," her mother says, pointing to the lit coil on the console. Annie's is only around the corner, the woods cutting the one house off from the row of ranches. The road used to go to Saxonburg until they put the reservoir in. Sometimes Melvina thinks she would like the privacy, except the county doesn't plow it. She turns in, and the water tank looms, giant, blue.

"Mother, you're going to have to sit on the hump."

"Is that her?" her mother asks.

Melvina sees her waving by the mailbox, coat half-zipped, hair a tangle, flat on one side. Jerrell is always asking Melvina why she bothers, the girl is trouble, anyone can see that.

"Oh," Melvina says, "and how do you see trouble?"

"Shit," Jerrell says, "you just look. There it is — trouble."

"You don't even know her," she says. "She's very nice." But Annie is not very nice, is not a friend like the one Melvina imagined when Mrs. Peterson's family decided to take her to Florida with them. She is young in all the wrong ways; she never knows when to stop. She treated Glenn like trash, for Brock, and from what Melvina has seen (and sometimes she likes what she sees: Brock doesn't worry about the oil bill, he likes the night life, the strip above the old Armco works), Brock isn't the marrying kind. Like Jerrell, she asks herself what Annie could possibly be getting out of it. Her answer changes when Jerrell collapses on her, sour-breathed from his three beers watching the Penguins, musky from climbing all day. He is a lineman for the phone company, and at times Melvina dreams of dialing a fatal number, a bolt of energy that will reach him wherever he is around the county and knock him, safety belt and all, senseless through the wires. She loves him, she supposes, or else why would she still be here — and where else would she go? But thinking like this is silly; she is not going anywhere. She does love the idiot. She is not perfect. She would have settled for Glenn.

Amy stands over the spillway, watching the pond seep beneath the ice, the dark, caught bubbles. Where do the fish go? She reaches down and feels how hard the ice is, how stuck. But on the other side of the plank, water splashes cold over the sluice. It is snowing and she sees she has lost a mitten. From the hill comes the shudder and whine of trucks on the highway. She takes her other mitten off and drops it over the edge, where it disappears under the silver gush, then forms again, pink, beneath the ice.

Hot August, Annie's father would take her fishing out at the reservoir. He had a glazed ceramic jar with a lid she'd made for him in art in which he'd grind out his Lucky Strikes. When the jar was full they called it a day. She has pictures stuck in her mirror of herself standing on the concrete launch, holding a stringer of perch, crappie, a lucky trout. Just her, her brothers were too old for that. "The hell with them," her father used to say, lounging on the cooler, an orange life preserver behind his head, "they wouldn't know a good time if it bit them square in the behind."

She refused to see him in the hospital; on the phone she said she would see him when he got home.

"Don't wait too long for me," he said, his voice rags.

"Do you want me to come in?" she asked.

"I think you'd better," he said.

"Did you hear that?" her mother said from the kitchen extension.

"I heard it!"

"I don't want you two fighting," her father said, so they fought in the car.

Melvina takes the dirt road down along the tree line, bumping over the frozen, rutted mud.

"I don't think the car is built for this," her mother says.

"Look don't talk," Melvina says. The fields are empty, last year's late corn cropped in rows, a few bent and bleached survivors waving limply. The radio is on to get the weather; the real snow is still holding off, it is too cold yet. At the corner of the field, a dirt mound sprouting a few old fenceposts blocks the road.

"Too many parties," Melvina says, and puts it into park.

"I'll stay here," her mother says. Annie is already out and headed down toward the pond.

"Give a honk every few minutes. That way we can't get lost."

"Roger wilco."

Melvina runs to catch up.

For the third time that week Glenn is late, and Wetmer calls him in at break. It is not really an office, just four partitions set down in the middle of the shop. Steel banging into scrap bins and the crackle of welding come through the open top. Wetmer has his jacket off and his sleeves rolled up like he is working, but he has the *Bradford Era* laid out on his desk, a cup of coffee sitting in the funnies. He doesn't look up while he talks.

"I hope this late thing has nothing to do with personal problems," he says.

"No, sir."

"You're paid to be here at seven sharp, you understand that."

"Yes, sir."

"You drink a little."

"No, sir."

"Let's keep it that way." He raises a hand to dismiss him.

Later, in the bathroom, Glenn slams the towel dispenser. "Fucking prick!"

"Who," Rafe asks from a stall, "Wetmer?"

"How come he's not busting your balls? You're late every time I am."

"It was your turn. Last time it was mine; next time it'll be mine again."

"Wrong," Wetmer says from another stall, "there isn't going to be no next time. Both of you dumbfucks are going to be out on your asses."

Regina, Melvina's mother, looks at her watch. They have only been gone a few minutes, but she expects them to appear at the end of the trail at any second, carrying a tearful Amy. It is amazing to her that something like this hasn't happened already, the way the girl lives. Cast the first stone and all, but in this case, the woman is an outright tramp, sleeping around on her husband and then taking up with a no-good. And from a perfectly nice family, that's the terrible thing. What her mother must go through every time she thinks of her. She knows May Pratt for a good woman. How her daughter turned out this way is a mystery, an honest-to-goodness shame. Regina hopes it is a black sheep thing, a wild gene, that Amy will turn out a Pratt. And who knows, this thing could teach Annie a lesson, turn her around. It is not the just man but the sinner God rejoices in saving. The forecast calls for 3 to 6 inches, 6 to 8 in the mountains. Regina checks her watch, reaches over, and honks the horn.

"Mom?" Amy calls from the kitchen, "can I have a red jelly bean?"

"No." Annie and Brock are watching "Wheel of Fortune."

"Please can I have one?"

"No, because you didn't finish your dinner."

"Oh, give her one."

"No. She didn't eat her dinner, why should she have candy?" She scans the letters and spaces but nothing comes. "You better not be eating jelly beans out there."

"Would she?" Brock asks.

"In a minute. Amy?" she calls, "Amy?" She gets up and finds Amy under the kitchen table, her cheeks crammed, a black string of drool on her chin. "Come out here now," Annie says. "Now! You come when I say!" She yanks her out by the arm, and Amy's head hits the bottom of the table. Amy begins to bawl, red-faced, showing the black candy cud. Annie spanks her and she chokes, then in one heave vomits everything she has in her stomach. "Goddammit, you little fuck."

"Hold on," Brock says, "hold on."

"You stay the fuck out of this," she says, pointing. Amy's face is red and ugly with fat tears. Her lip quivers as she tries to get her breath back. "Go watch your goddamn show," Annie says, and he does.

The path turns as it climbs. It is icy, and several times Annie falls hard. She looks back over the pond, the water tower rising over the wood, the fields to the north. Flakes drift down, drawn sharp by the dark, solid sky. Far off, white ranches shine, barns lean. The tamed fairways of the country club surround the turreted stone clubhouse, the emptied pool a blue dot. She has never been this far back, though she has known of the shortcut since middle school, and the view makes everything seem even stranger. She spots Melvina's green-and-black mackinaw in the brush below the spillway. The horn sounds, distant through the trees. There is no way Amy could make it up this, she thinks, but she keeps climbing, falling and getting up again as the whoosh and rush of the highway nears.

"Want to watch HBO?" Alicia asks, naked, sipping wine from the tiny sanitized glass. They have the beds pushed together, the heat blasting, and the lights out; sun sneaks in around the blinds, and when someone passes outside, shadows ripple across the back wall.

"There's never anything on in the day," Brock says. He tongues her navel, trying to get her to spill. She throws the cupful over him, and he yelps, then, laughing, dives across her and grabs the bottle off the nightstand.

"Don't waste it."

"We've got another."

"Let's not make a mess," she says. "Someone has to clean these rooms."

"How about the tub?" Brock suggests.

Annie scissors over the guardrail. A shred of truck tire lies on the gravel berm. The two sets of lanes are salt-stained, the snow in the dip of the median gray but virgin. She walks against traffic toward an overpass — Burdon Hollow Road, likely. A semi passes in the right lane, and the wind following knocks her back a step, gravel peppers her shins. A bleached beer case, a few wrenched and flattened pipes, rusting. Over the guardrail, the embankment is sheer now, the treetops at eye level. Annie looks down. Twenty feet below her, stuck in a crotch, sags a dead deer.

"What about taking me to Overlook?"

"I can't leave her alone like this," Melvina says. "I'll run you over when her young man gets here."

"Her young man," Regina mocks.

"Mother, don't you understand what is happening?"

"Yes, I'm missing my Thursday. But don't mind me. Maybe one of these policemen could ride me over."

"I think they have something a little more important to do."

"Excuse me, sir?"

"Mother, please."

"I'm just asking the young man."

"What can I do for you, ma'am?"

"See, he's not too busy for an old lady."

Wetmer calls him on the horn, and Rafe looks over from his rollaway like this might be it. Glenn leaves his gloves on the bench, wipes his hands on the backs of his thighs as he heads for the office. He answers a few stares with a shrug. It's not going to be a raise.

Wetmer looks him in the face and asks him to sit. "I got a call from the police," he says, and explains what they said. "You'd better get home now. Get one of your buddies to lock up for you, I'll punch you out."

Glenn sits there shaking his head. It is some kind of prank.

"Marchand, you all right? You gonna need a driver?"

"No."

"Then go," Wetmer says, "get home. Your wife needs you."

May grabs a tupperware carton of barley soup from the deep freeze in the basement, two twenties she keeps in her old teapot, and her purse, and is out the door and on the road. She pictures Amy in her powder blue jacket with the fur-trimmed hood, wandering in a wood—when that is the best thing that can happen. She tries not to think of a van slowing and stopping, a pair of hands. Or Amy on the ground, twigs caught in her white tights. "Goddammit," she yells at a red light, "let's go!"

Annie wakes on her bed with her clothes on, her boots off. Gray light fights through the plastic; the room looks tired, the clothes in a heap, the scattered toys. Talk seeps in from the kitchen.

"Brock," she calls.

There is a knock, and then a policewoman looks in. "Your husband is on the way. Can I get you anything?"

"What husband?" she says. "Where's Amy?"

"We have people out, and we'll have the Lifeflight helicopter from Kersey in a few minutes. We're trying to do everything. Do you want to go out? I'm supposed to accompany you if you do. My name is Officer Scott."

"Where's Brock?"

Roy Barnum walks into the Marigold, takes a stool and orders decaf, milk and sugar. He's on duty and it's free, Grant's rule. Karleen draws it off the urn, clanks it down. Roy slides a flier across the counter, a Polaroid print taped to the paper, a little girl in a snowsuit, puffy cheeks, devilish smile. "Put this up in a good spot for me?" Roy asks, but Karleen has seen the name, and one hand covering her mouth, stands speechless.

The road is lined with police cars — some state, Brock sees — and, quickly weighing turning around, he parks under the water tower and hurries over the snow. A burglar maybe. He imagines he will be heartbroken if Annie is dead, but in time recover. The house is full of cops. Glenn is there, and asks where the fuck he has been.

"Work," Brock says.

"Amy is missing," Annie's mother says as if it is his fault. He wonders if they can smell the soap on him, the wine through his gum. Amy is missing. Nothing in the world goes right for him.

"Are you the boyfriend?" a cop asks.

"Where's Annie?" Brock asks.

The snow comes down sideways, blowing, smoothing over footprints in minutes. The Lifeflight is grounded. There is only another hour of light, and it is already poor. The woods crackle with volunteers — the Thursday AA meeting is here, the Methodist Women's Alliance. Melvina and Jerrell search the cannibalized pickups and tractors at the north edge of the cornfield; Annie, Brock, and Glenn are with the sheriff down below the pond. May and Regina talk in Annie's living room, the weather channel on silently beside them. Grant has taped Amy's flier to the front door of the Marigold, closed up, and driven out with Karleen — him in his apron under his jacket, her in uniform, bare legs, heels and all. The hunt has spread across the interstate to the middle school grounds; trucks file by the flares, the troopers' orange-coned flashlights. The Army Reserve has promised several squads if this should go till tomorrow.

Yet it will not be any of these searchers who finds Amy, but a fourteen-year-old Boy Scout, small for his size, generally picked on, named Arthur Parkinson, who, because she is dead, will not be a hero — will not, years from now, even be mentioned around town as the one who found her — but who, with Annie and Glenn and Brock and May and Melvina and Karleen, will find Amy again and again throughout his life and never ever lose her.

Mr. Wu Thinks

This is what I think, Mr. Wu thinks, because he is thinking in English, an exercise his night-school instructor suggests at the end of each class. This is what I think, he thinks, as if preparing an essay, sliding cigarettes into their slots, his hands dancing sure between boxes and cartons and packs. He thinks it again, a phrase longing for clauses of insight; but when Mr. Wu really thinks, he thinks in Cantonese with English brand names inserted. There aren't enough characters for his merchandise. Popular brands — Marlboro, Michelob — have their own invented characters, but even these he marks with proper names on invoices and order forms.

Lately, when serving customers, he grades his remarks and tries to catch mistakes. The regulars — some college students, Mr. Ridley, Mrs. Winningham and her dog Bugs — encourage him, praising "Right away" and "It is not here today" with polite, childish wonder. Mr. Wu understands their concern while noting in it a kind condescension. None of them says, "Learn the language," but he has overheard others. He realizes the importance of mastering this new system of communication and the effort he alone must make. When business is slow, he reads magazines, and twice a week, Wednesdays and Fridays, he attends "English as a Second Language" at Brighton High. Friends coaxed him to the class a year ago, and though some have passed and joined more complex courses given by local universities, they still get together and read Thursday nights.

Mrs. Wu thinks he's crazy, a grown man picking through a third grader's spelling book, mouthing words, coming home with his pockets full of paper scraps, asking his sons schoolboy questions. She tells him, "Let the children take care of it. In a year you'll retire, you'll never have to speak English again." But he continues with his studies, sometimes late into the night at the desk in their room.

His sons, Lee and Tommy, approve. We're Americans, they both say, and considering their lives, Mr. Wu agrees. Twenty years in Boston, Lee three years at Digital, wife, house, new car; Tommy at U Mass–Harborside, majoring in sociology. Mr. Wu remembers childhood episodes: Lee at twelve playing in his first snow, Tommy bicycling around the parking lot. In the back closet, Mrs. Wu has organized their old toys — primary-colored plastics, fluorescent tennis balls, day-glo skateboards. When he opens the door, the past jumps out with cartoon clarity. But Mr. Wu knows the problems they have had, the "gooks" and "dinks" and "chinks." Huddled over his spelling book, he sometimes sees them as heroic, besieged by troubles. Although Tommy has been out of the apartment only a year, he has grown into a legend, a bright memoir Mrs. Wu is tiring of.

Sunday nights the five of them eat dinner together, either in or at a restaurant. The conversation slips in and out of Cantonese, making Mrs. Wu nervous. The rest worry about her. They imagine her unable to communicate; they forget Mr. Wu has just begun to speak English. When a phrase eludes him, he shakes his head, and Anne, Lee's wife, translates for him. He orders steak and mashed potatoes until he learns fried chicken; then pork chops, fried shrimp, peas. At home he names Mrs. Wu's dishes. The section in his notebook labeled *Food* thickens.

They talk of Lee's promotion, Tommy's classes, Anne's new car. Having lived in cities all their lives, Mr. and Mrs. Wu absorb Anne's description of Waltham, stopping her when they don't understand. "And the car," Mr. Wu asks, "you like it?" Mr. Wu has never driven; he rides his bike everywhere. But now, the move to Waltham assured, he thinks he should learn. He asks Lee.

"Ask her," he says, "it's her car."

Anne agrees and sets a date. Saturday she'll pick him up and take him out on Route 1. He can practice in the lot behind Digital.

On Tuesday, Mrs. Wu asks him if she can come. Delighted, Mr. Wu takes her to the Volkswagen dealer in Allston. They read brochures and gesture with the salesmen, check prices. With their present savings buying a car is impossible, but when they move in with Lee and Anne . . .

Afterward, they go to Shanghai Gardens in Brookline. They talk with Mr. Lin, the owner, while they wait for their food. Mr. Lin is in Mr. Wu's class and tries to speak English whenever possible. Tonight, in deference to Mrs. Wu, he speaks in dialect. "Sounds like you're ready to retire," he kids Mr. Wu.

"Soon I will be ready."

"And me," adds Mrs. Wu in English.

In class Wednesday, Mr. Wu sits beside Mrs. Aliviera, a small brunette troubled by silent "e." As Mr. Wu answers question after question—although the semester has just started, he is already studying for the midterm—she smiles at him, one hand crumpled around a pen, a dark line in the open *V* of her blouse shifting like the needle of a gauge. "That is the modifier, sir," he answers, but his foot, he notices, veers off to the right. At first he wonders why. He has been attracted to other women before, but never this dangerously. Is she serious? Has she approached him before? Involuntarily, facts and possibilities arise. Her husband has left her; she has one small boy and rents on Glenville. She must have been looking past him. For the last twenty minutes of class he watches her feet.

At home that night Mrs. Wu pampers him. It is a hard day, she thinks, working all day at the store and then at class all night. She strips his clothes off and fetches a bowl of cold soup. In shorts he sits on the old couch in the living room, his feet propped on the coffee table. A fan in the doorway pushes hot air across his chest.

They watch television before bed. As police fire into curtained windows, Mr. Wu describes his day. He feels guilty for leaving Mrs. Wu alone, so that instead of studying, he spends forty-five minutes discussing candy bars, Mrs. Winningham and Bugs, deliveries — details of any Wednesday. Mrs. Wu has heard it before but still enjoys his stories. Is it her imagination, or is he more eloquent tonight? They smile and laugh, comforted by routine.

But Mr. Wu, thinking of Mrs. Aliviera, wishes Mrs. Wu would go to bed. As she speaks, he watches her eyes, the words passing through him. He nods and smiles, returns her gaze, his mind a list compiling. After a while she picks up her slippers and warns him, "Don't stay up too late. You need to sleep too."

He collects his books and sits down at the desk. Under the covers Mrs. Wu sighs. He clicks off the overhead light and turns on the desk lamp. Giant shadows of his hands menace the walls.

First, the words. He copies a column of "-ight" words: "fight, flight, fright, night, right," then folds the page over and copies them on the other side, again and again until he has them memorized. To avoid waking Mrs. Wu, he closes the bathroom door before saying them aloud to the mirror. Improvising gestures for each word, he turns out the light, turns it on again, raises his eyebrows, wiggles his elbows up and down. Memory, his instructor says each class, memory is knowledge. Mr. Wu watches himself smile "ight."

All morning he thinks of tonight's homework help session. In the walk-in, rearranging the frozen foods, he divides the day into four sections: work, dinner, homework, and sleep. Later, in the middle of reading *Life* at the counter, he stops and plots the day on paper, filling time slots with red, green, blue, and yellow magic marker. Next to each chore he draws a star. He realizes it is unnecessary — he can shop without a list, remember appointments weeks ahead — but, hoping to make room for English, he purges his mind. On paper, in cramped, childish print, his life appears as simple as a recipe.

Around noon, customers start piling in for tonic, chips, and sandwiches. Mr. Wu jerks the slicer back and forth. He has set the blade level at an eighth of an inch. Four slices equal a quarter-pound. The lettuce, onions, and tomatoes lie in plastic tubs on the counter, letting him make any sandwich, any combination, in less than a minute. The line at the register moves but stays three deep. Practiced fingers play the register; the other hand slides cans along. He makes change by touch. He works faster now, spearing cigarettes, slapping mustard on buns, wrapping, bagging, ringing. The Foodstop Corporation rewards his performance. Every week Mr. Wu makes fifty dollars more than any other Food-stop clerk. His evaluation invariably reads, "Highly motivated," and each year they name him Employee of the Month once or twice. Last year when they asked him if he would speak at their annual awards dinner, he declined. He has thought of giving a speech this year (the new February plaque hangs by the Pepsi clock) but doubts they will ask again. As he takes care of the stragglers, he slows, as if the number of customers determines his speed. Finally, the last nickel deposit returned, lunch ends.

In the afternoon Mr. Wu circles words he doesn't know in magazines, then reads the *Globe* and the *New York Times* to keep up with the world. At two he crosses *Work* off his list. He pays himself for a Coke and reads another magazine.

Half an hour before quitting time Mrs. Winningham pushes into the store, dragging fat, sad-faced Bugs by his leash. "Hel-lo, Mr. Wu," she says. "And how are you to-day?" Her face wrinkles with each exaggerated word.

"I am OK, Mrs. Winningham. And you are?" It is from the first class, page one in his notes.

"I am fine." She hesitates. "Thank you."

"You are welcome." Mr. Wu thinks his first reflexive thought in English, advice from his instructor: she means well. Excited but cautious, he says, "I am glad you came."

"Why, thank you."

"You are welcome." Shouldn't have said it again, he thinks in

Cantonese, and then, the triumph still fresh, ushers them into the back for Bugs's daily treat.

At dinner Mr. and Mrs. Wu argue.

"You said later this year," Mrs. Wu says over the steaming chicken. "You said we'd be moved in by winter."

"I said I was thinking of retiring."

She picks at it with her fork.

"What am I supposed to do," Mr. Wu asks, "quit?" He puts his napkin on the table; it recoils under his hand. "Well?"

"You're supposed to relax. We have enough money to retire. Lee has a good job, and Tommy's almost done with school. You don't have to work yourself into the grave."

"We'll talk about this later," Mr. Wu says. "This is ruining my dinner."

Dropped. Forgotten. Mrs. Wu digs into her chicken breast. Mr. Wu shoves the napkin back in his lap, and they eat, clinking.

At first Mr. Wu believes Mrs. Aliviera is late, but as the instructor pairs the students off, he realizes she isn't coming. Mr. Lin, now enrolled in Northeastern's restaurant management program, helps Mr. Wu with his homework. They run through irregular verbs, Mr. Wu taking notes as Mr. Lin conjugates. Around the room, a high-ceilinged hall filled with pool tables and air hockey games, groups of two huddle over books. From the second floor come the squeaks and thunder of a basketball game. Lee and Tommy played here. In the main hall, behind heavy glass, their names gleam on cast-bronze-and-marble trophies. As Mr. Lin recites, Mr. Wu remembers his sons standing thin and long-muscled as the anthem played. Mr. Lin taps his notebook. "Drink, drank, drunk," he says.

"Drink, drank, drunk," Mr. Wu says.

After the session the instructor stays to talk with Mr. Wu. He has noticed his progress and wonders if he is too advanced for the class. He suggests a night course at Boston University, "Basic Compositional Skills." What does Mr. Wu think? Mr. Wu answers with a shrug, not knowing if he is ready for such a big step. He has been studying hard, and his homeworks have been perfect, but he sees himself as part of the class, not the head. Telling him to take his time (but the session starts in two weeks), the instructor hands him a brochure.

A year before, faced with the same question, Mr. Wu would have abstained and finished the class; now, before he reaches home, before he even opens the brochure, he says yes. Once home, he goes immediately to bed. Mrs. Wu does not ask what's wrong.

Over breakfast the Wus reconcile, conferring in slower, softer voices. Seeing Mr. Wu worn and tired, though no different from any other morning, Mrs. Wu decides to give him more time. In his pajamas, his hair morning-mussed, he looks like a teenager too tall for his weight. He pours himself a second cup of coffee as she clears the table, drinks it on his way to the shower.

Friday is always busy. People stock up for the weekend, remember items while driving back from the supermarket. In the early afternoon, students empty the ice machine, filling stolen shopping carts. They ravage the snack shelves, buy out the beer. Amid the frenzy, Mr. Wu studies automotive magazines. The intricate engines impress him, but there are no instructions, not even hints on driving. He covers a page and a half with new words, promising himself to ask Anne what they mean. Mrs. Winningham and Bugs visit; Mr. Ridley, the super at Chiswick Towers around the corner, stops in for a pony beer. At five, when he sums the day's receipts and hands the keys over to the swing man, Mr. Wu feels ready for bed.

After a calm supper, Mr. Wu attends class. Again, Mrs. Aliviera is absent, but Mr. Wu, more confused by his own presence — there is no reason for him to be here, yet he is furiously taking notes — notes the empty chair without emotion. It should bother him, the loss of tense meetings for coffee, the shadowed rooms of Glenville Street, but to him the affair has already occurred, become a future memory. Now, the instructor scratching at the board, Mr. Wu can think of only tomorrow's driving lesson. His pen moves, a simple recorder.

Class over, the instructor and Mr. Wu discuss the advanced course. Many of the words the instructor uses Mr. Wu does not know, but unable to stanch the flow of congratulations, Mr. Wu nods and smiles, listening intently so as not to miss the time, date, and place. Tuition, which Mr. Wu has so far ignored, must be paid in advance. The instructor gives him another brochure on financial aid. "Do you have any questions?" he asks.

"No," Mr. Wu says.

The instructor rises, Mr. Wu rises, and they shake hands. "I'm giving you an *A* for the term. I'll mail you a card." He puts on his coat, grabs his briefcase, and heads for the hallway.

"Thank you," Mr. Wu calls after him.

"Take care now."

Mr. Wu watches him go, the midterm vanished, then collects his notebooks and walks the long, echoing hall. The janitor locks the front doors behind him.

Walking home slowly, he thinks about Waltham, about retirement. The streets are humid after a shower, and he folds his jacket over his arm. His age, Mrs. Wu, the apartment, Tommy, Lee, Anne — everything seems related, no single thing dominates, so that instead of weighing the family's hopes against his own fears, he concentrates on the literal changes the move will bring. He enjoys the city, the rush of life always a door away. He has traveled through the country, though fewer times than he now remembers, and like most city people sees it as a vacation, a quiet replaced within a week by the screaming real life of the streets. And he has passed through the suburbs, but so briefly that his memory remits only fragments, trees and shopping centers and roads, landscapes emptied of people. He walks on, the silhouettes of hanging plants and curtains soothing him. For twenty minutes he has walked and thought, but only now, fitting his key into the building's outer door, Mrs. Wu waiting for him upstairs, does he decide to decide.

Mrs. Wu snores, the back-rush and whistle as light and steady as the ticking of a metronome. Above her breathing, Mr. Wu's pen rolls a fugue. Before him lies a page, right side headed "Boston," left "Waltham." For five lines he manages counterpoint, then slips into monody. He scans the list, doodling. Giant hands menace.

Both Mr. and Mrs. Wu are up when Anne buzzes. Mrs. Wu makes bacon and eggs and toast, Mr. Wu's favorite breakfast. They eat quickly, Anne having only toast, telling them how simple the car is to drive, the options included in the list price, and several other items Mr. Wu immediately memorizes. While Mrs. Wu hunts for her blue dress — worn every special occasion — Mr. Wu and Anne do the dishes.

Anne explains the differences between standards and automatics and why she chose the latter. "I like to have my hands free for coffee or the radio," she says. They are sitting in the parking lot of Digital Electronics, the big mirrored block-and-ell throwing a wavy red Toyota back across the asphalt. Anne shifts into *D* and the car rolls forward, into *N* and it coasts, the motor murmuring. She traces figure eights over the numbered spaces, forward, backward, forward. In the backseat Mrs. Wu laughs. Mr. Wu watches Anne's hands on the wheel, her feet on the pedals. After a review of the signals and lights ("Is it safe to drive at night?" Mrs. Wu asks), Anne jerks the emergency brake up, removes her safety belt, and steps out. "Come on," she says, "don't be afraid."

It is all decided, he thinks, releasing the emergency brake. He is pleased it is over, the waiting. They will move at the end of August, before winter. Tommy will take care of the store. Class will be over by then.

Anne reaches over and shifts into *D* and the car inches forward. Mr. Wu stares through the windshield, his arms straight and stiff, feet flat on the floor. Overhead, gulls wheel. Why so far inland?

"Give it some gas," Anne says.

He responds.

The Doctor's Sickness

Doctor Markham loved Monday morning and the start of another workweek. One eye closed by his pillow, he remembered business he had left hanging Friday and arranged his coming day. Downstairs, his housekeeper Mrs. Railsbeck was sautéing margarine for his one over-easy, the radio on higher than it need be to wake him. Even her Muzak couldn't discourage him. Monday! He pitched out of bed, tossing the covers behind him, and glanced off the bathroom door frame. He made a practice of not lingering on the pot, though the *Geographic* piece on the endangered African elephant attracted him. Monday, the weekend's lethargy lifting like a wet fog, invigorating as the cold shower he drew, flooding him with names of patients, forms half-filled and waiting, yellow tabs by the missing information. The people he would see today!

Yes, yes, yes, yes, yes, he would see her — blonde girl, make-up, terminal, a shame. Was it today or next Monday? Never mind, today he was bound to have a full slate. Flu season. Plus, plus — what? Lord, what was happening to his memory? He groped for the washrag hanging on the showerhead, swabbed his face, whipped the curtain aside, and climbed out. Through the crack in the door, he could see Mrs. Railsbeck making his bed.

She watched him eat, trying to force a second piece of toast on him, another glass of the white grape juice he didn't like in the first place. She seemed disappointed, and he made up for it by promising to have something at coffee break. He never did; she'd given up asking when he got home. It was a ritual, and out of courtesy he deferred to her. If Helen were alive, he imagined he would be doing the same for her. He left her to do the dishes and went upstairs for the tie and handkerchief she had laid out for him. He was two minutes ahead of schedule when he went downstairs to get his hat and coat and gloves before starting out for Utica, forty miles away.

Doctor Markham drove a Chrysler Imperial, forest green, with a white landau roof. The odometer, which in the course of the doctor's ministering to parts of three towns had rolled over twice, now read a constant 70,153 miles. The commute was one of the job's few drawbacks. In private practice, the doctor had covered upwards of three hundred miles a week, but driving the same route over and over at the same time every day, half of it creeping along the Thruway in rush hour traffic, he could not get used to. He was afraid the city driving was hurting the Imperial. It was idling higher, he could hear it at lights. Now that Junie was gone, his place on Main boarded up, the doctor often took the Rabbit he'd bought for Mrs. Railsbeck, and left her the big car for around town, knowing she would never use it. This on nice days; when it was raining or snowing, or threatening to, Doctor Markham made the commute to Utica in style, trying not to worry about the wear and tear, the gallons the big V-8 gulped down.

This morning, it was sleeting, treacherous, and the doctor could see himself in the Rabbit, tucked under the grille of a cement mixer. Monday seemed to call for the plush silence of the Chrysler, the news nattering away beneath the heater's whir. He pinched off one glove, put the Rabbit's keys in the nut dish they used for the paperboy's stubs, and began to search his pockets.

"Gray coat," Mrs. Railsbeck called from the kitchen sink, "right front-hand pocket, where you always keep them," and came steaming up the hall, wiping her hands on her apron. He stepped aside to let her at the closet. "Here," she said, "now how about a hat?"

He touched his head. He was sure he'd had one on.

She fixed his brim. "You're gorgeous," she said, and steered him to the door.

Up 17 to 27, 27 to the Thruway, the Thruway in. He got the heater going and fell into the flow of the road, Doughty Creek snaking along on his right, looping wide then hugging a curve. Snow sat on rocks in midstream. There was nothing to see. The woods were empty this time of year, the farmers kept their herds inside; the cows watched TV—or so the TV people would have you think. TV, that's what it would come to. The black-and-white weekends were starting to get to him, cooped up in the house with her. Purgatory, he imagined, would be a living room at four in the afternoon in winter, gray fading grayer, a pendulum clock in the next room, her forever reading a mystery novel under an amber lamp shade. On TV would be Ronald Coleman, John Garfield, George Raft. That's what he had to look forward to, and soon.

Friday, Reynard had asked him if he had considered retiring. It was a complete surprise to the doctor, and Reynard had to calm him down. No one was forcing him out, any action was voluntary, any decision his. Reynard had asked to be the one to ask him, usually they sent a formal letter. The budget crunch was on, across the board, and Reynard was feeling people out on his own. He didn't want to let anyone go who wasn't prepared.

"Who else have you approached with this?" Doctor Markham asked.

"Understand, I have to come to you first."

"Why?"

"Why," Reynard said, "because you're seventy-six years old, Bill, why the hell do you think?"

Doctor Markham hadn't had to remind Reynard that he wasn't far behind him.

He couldn't think of anything he'd done wrong. Yet it had to be something he'd done, or not done, the way he'd handled a patient maybe.

The girl screaming at him the other day was nothing out of the ordinary. He'd done it himself, alone in his office at home, raging at the flimsy test result—and at sixty-five. He was worried she would give up too soon, and was relieved when she blew up at him. Her file said she'd been through it before, but that was no guarantee. It seemed to him that people nowadays, as opposed to when he was a young man, simply didn't have as much gumption. Hardly a week passed when the clinic didn't have at least one case of nervous exhaustion. At first meeting, the girl seemed the type, thin as a rake, hair dyed, make-up troweled on. (Lithuanian nationalists sustained heavy casualties in the ongoing battle for Vilnius, the radio quoted Tass.) Was that her? His memory had been playing tricks on him lately. It was the reason he'd asked for more tests on the girl: he couldn't be sure the first set were actually hers. There could have been some confusion with the patient roster, either that or the prints had gotten mixed up in processing, because a second set for her permanent file showed nothing. That might have been enough for someone internal to lodge a complaint.

He blamed Reynard. They were Easties when that had meant something in Tindalls Corners. As boys, they had chased each other through the gap in Mrs. Haabestaad's hedgerow, winging rocks and crab apples at each other. His entire schooling Reynard was a year behind him, a chum but a hothead, and countless times Bill Markham had come to his aid on the playground, glowering, arms folded, daring the West End tough who'd been ready to plant Rey to give it a try. At Colgate they drifted apart, found different crowds to run with, Rey's wild, engineers aiming for the Army Air Corps, his the more genteel medical students, but even as upstanding interns Rey would punch him in the arm as he passed in the hall. Rey drew the South Pacific, Doctor Markham Fort Sill, and after they saw each other seldom. Forty years, yet when the doctor called five years ago, Rey hadn't forgotten.

He hadn't now either, he was only being fair to the young people. The doctor shifted on the bench seat, both hands on the wheel. How had he become so old?

The road twisted up a hill. In the hollow below to his right shone the bright swatches of an auto graveyard. The Imperial could use a new odometer. It was illegal, but the stuck one bothered him. He'd stop in next Saturday, make a day of installing it in the garage. Ahead of him, a coal truck pulled half onto the berm to let him pass, but the doctor couldn't see around him. A pickup behind him honked. Why hadn't he noticed the junkyard before? He drove the road every day. Coming home he might not see it down in the hollow, but in the morning it would be hard to miss. The pickup honked; Doctor Markham waved. It was a double yellow line, they were going uphill and the road was all curves.

Really though, it was something that would catch his eye, especially in winter, that burst of color. How would the Imperial look in red or lemon yellow? The pickup honked again and shot into the left lane, the driver, a man with a dark mustache, turning to look at him and giving him a look as he passed, then gunning around the coal truck, spraying cinders.

"Nut," the doctor muttered.

He had never seen the auto graveyard before, he realized after clearing the rise and waiting for the coal truck to turn into a fenced depot, because it was not Route 17 he was on but some other road. He had missed a turn, maybe taken a wrong turn shadowing the truck. How far he had gone on the new road he could not tell, but the surroundings were completely foreign. "Shawcross," the trucking company's sign read, the word ominous, as if whispered. A sense of déjà vu came over him. The radio was going to say, "under the new coalition government," just as it said, "the new coalition government," and the road sign which assured him he was on Route 17 slid past with the woods behind it as it had for years, months, days. It was only 7:20, he couldn't have gone far past the turnoff. He would T-bone some other road, but for the life of him he couldn't think what road that would be. He was on 17 and he wanted to be on 17 before the turnoff, that's all he knew. Driving straight ahead, he felt he was getting himself more lost. He would stop at the next place to stop and check a map.

The speed limit changed to 40, and a group of buildings formed in the distance, a gas station, he would stop there. A tree of signs said it was the junction of 17 and 27. He pulled in short of the station and, in park, shuffled his maps. There was one of Pennsylvania, one of New York, and one of New Jersey. He did not know which one he was in.

"Curious," he said. He got out and checked his license plate, got back in and found 17 on the New York map, and when he saw the yellow blotch of Utica remembered hesitantly who he was and where he was going and realized what had happened.

He found a red Flair and marked his route on the map, and to make sure, wrote his name. He propped the map on the dash, remembering at the last second to fasten his seat belt, and turned onto 27, heading for Utica, still on time.

Fugue. He'd seen all kinds. Medics rotated back to Fort Sill to be demobbed and ended up taking a bed, lying silent for weeks then suddenly asking for a cigarette. A woman they found wandering outside Hecla thought she'd died and gone to another world; her boyfriend made his own wheat beer and a batch of mash must have had ergot in it–LSD. Stroke, the thin wall popping, brain tumor, epilepsy, there were any number of ways to explain it. His little episode didn't seem serious. But he could not deny that he had had one.

Friday, Reynard had asked him if he'd thought of retiring. They'd grown up together, and this was the way the man treated him. How many times had he saved his hide when they were flyers that one summer, shuddering over the unlit washboard roads through farms, bottles clinking fit to bust because the Canadians gypped them on excelsior. But there came a time, the doctor had to admit. Television, murder mysteries. He killed the news.

He was on time, which meant he would be the first one in. He felt fine now, the connections sparking from the clinic's windows, the clock tower opposite, the tamed shrubbery leading to the doors. The security guard wore a name tag but Doctor Markham knew Keith Coles. In uniform, a toothpick sticking out one corner of his mouth, Keith looked like a sleazy movie sheriff. He'd been studying for the civil service exams for months, taking them over and over, never giving up. His persistence reminded the doctor of Susanna's ex-husband Darcy, not knowing when to quit with his music. He'd spend the rent to record a demo tape without asking her. The man was in his thirties and hadn't had a real job in his life. But every letter Sue sent made it clearer that she regretted the divorce.

"What's going on, Doc?" Keith asked.

"Monday."

"Tell me about it."

Thursday morning Keith had been talking about going ice-fishing up at Echo Lake. The doctor asked, testing.

"What are you, kidding me? Go up this time a year you'll be swimming."

"Anyone in?"

"Yeah, right," Keith said, "you're the only crazy one."

Alone in back, Doctor Markham read the nameplate on the desk of the work-study girl and in his office wrote it down on a Travenol pad. His desk calendar said he had a full slate, the morning splitting walk-in with Doctor Kennedy, the afternoon handling paperwork, some dating from last year. It was a solid day. No matter what the university said, he was needed; Reynard would see that.

Doctor Markham took the first patient, a girl complaining of dizziness, nausea, and when it appeared that Doctor Kennedy was late, saw the second, no feeling in the fingertips, the third, vomiting, cramps, and by 9:30 Doctor Kennedy had called in sick and the waiting room was filling up with students who had waited all weekend to come in. There was a flu going around, and a chest cold brought on by a sudden temperature change. The doctor took them in order, cutting short their explanations, keeping the seats half-empty. Even with the automatic diagnoses of cold and flu, he was losing ground. He skipped break, later between flu victims bought an awful cup of coffee and leaden danish from the machines.

It would be then that Reynard Vaught chose to come out of his office to see how things were going. He caught Doctor Markham in the hall, chewing. "I hear you're minding the store yourself," he said. "If you need a hand, I can assign someone."

At 1:00, when Doctor Markham turned the walk-in over to Reynard and Doctor Downes, there were five people waiting. "If you need help," he said, "I'll be in my office."

He was only starting in on the mass of forms and memos that had built up when, hours later, he woke up in a nest of papers, one stem of his glasses cutting into his temple. Before leaving he had another cup of coffee, and that night went to bed early, dropping off in the middle of the *Geographic* article. The next morning, refreshed, he found the magazine closed on his bed stand, leafed to the page he had stopped on, and dog-eared it.

Half the staff were out with the flu, Reynard among them. Doctor Markham called him at home to see how he was doing. Reynard said he felt fine, then all of a sudden couldn't keep anything down. The doctor prescribed clear fluids and rest, told Reynard not to worry, he was minding the fort.

"Who's in charge?" Reynard asked.

"Someone with experience," the doctor said.

He fell asleep again Wednesday afternoon because he forgot to look at the index card in his pocket that said, "Eat Lunch." It was somehow worse than blanking out completely, the insidious erosion. Like the confusion of papers before him, his daily life was overwhelming him. He needed a guide like the map propped on the Imperial's dash, like the little yellow notes Mrs. Railsbeck stuck to the fridge—"waxed paper" or "nutmeg."

Exactly. She'd gotten hers from him. He raided the supply cabinet, and by the end of the day his blotter bore a fringe of messages, among the clutter invisible to all but him. One said, "Thurs. 11 A.M. Term Girl."

The next morning, Reynard was in. A formal letter had come. The university was cutting its facilities staff 3 percent across the board. They were offering their older employees retirement bonuses, trying to cut down by attrition so the layoff numbers looked better in the paper. The trustees were asking Reynard for one name.

"A week's pay for every year," Reynard told him. "Heck, I'm even tempted."

"I'm new, Rey."

"And you keep your benefits."

"I wouldn't know what to do with myself."

"Westmoreland always needs people." Reynard folded the letter. "You're not making this easy, Bill."

"Nope."

"Consider it, for me, please. It's the best deal you're going to get."

"Things happen."

"Why are you doing this to me? You know I'm not going to kick you out in the street. Why can't you take what they're giving?"

"Rey, go ahead and can me, I won't think badly of you."

"I don't want to can you, Bill. I don't want to can anyone. But understand, I don't have a choice. Someone is going to go, and from all evidence it's you. I'm just telling you the truth. You've been here five years and you've done good work, but I can't keep a place open for you anymore." He slapped the letter against his knee. "Bill."

"Is that it," the doctor asked, "can I get back to work now?"

"You have the rest of the semester to come to your senses."

The door hadn't closed when the work-study girl poked her head in—he could never remember her name—and told him there was a Janice Toth waiting.

It did not go well. She was more composed than before, or perhaps he was more distraught. He paced the perimeter of the office, gabbling, it seemed to him, out of control, while she sat in the chair Reynard had been in, watching him with the patience of a snake. Munson Hall's clock refused to strike the half hour. Telling her of the switched tests, he avoided any mention of his recent problems, and each time he turned to her, using the desk as a barrier, a prop, he would come face-to-face with "Eat Lunch," and the urge to confess set him off on another circuit of the room. At one point he knocked a sheaf of papers to the floor, laughed, and horrified, tried to cover it with a diatribe on the risk of swelling. Finally the bells chimed. Unfathomably hungry, he walked her out to Scott and left the two to set up a lab date.

Even a tuna melt couldn't keep him awake. He would never catch up on his paperwork. Maybe Reynard couldn't fire him until it was done. It wasn't Rey's fault, it wasn't anyone's. He'd had his day, no sense being a bad sport about it. He couldn't imagine Rey would go any easier. He'd always had to drag him off his opponent, or vice versa, grappling in the dirt outside the tent set up for dancing. Rey was a wild man then. It was the war, or maybe just the speed of his youth that took it out of him. He married, settled down in the city. The doctor had visited a few times but never felt comfortable. Then Helen, a new life, Susanna.

Wouldn't it be something to punch old Reynard Vaught smack in the kisser? For old times' sake. Boof — ha-ha — right in the jaw.

Driving home that night, the Imperial's right headlight burned out, leaving a single beam angling off into the ditch. He greeted Mrs. Railsbeck by demanding a yellow tab, which he filled out, "Junkyard 17" and stuck to the fridge.

"I'm taking the Rabbit tomorrow," he told her over dinner.

"I have shopping to do."

"The car does not bite," he said.

While she did the dishes, the doctor went into his office and emptied his briefcase. The terminal girl, for all his fear and pity of her, he considered his only real patient. He had asked her for her family doctor's file after the first scan, but it must have slipped her mind, for her folder held only two slips from the lab, both positive. The negative CAT plates were locked away in the clinic's files, evidence of his failing mind.

The girl was going to die, he had no doubts. How much agony or hope his mistake was putting her through he could not imagine. Helen had gone so quickly. It was irresponsible, it was malpractice—and yet he could not be sure it was his mistake or a mistake at all. Because he was rooting for her, a worse mistake, one he had problems with so many times in the past five years he did not want to recall. He was supposed to be beyond such hope, but with every new one it returned. The families invited him, he sent a card. Who would Reynard get for a job no one could do?

He finished the *Geographic* article in bed, pausing before the heaps of bloodied tusks, the government wardens with semiautomatics held across their chests. Everything was becoming extinct, the natives, the savannah, the elephants; it was every *Geographic* article he had ever read. Lying there in the dark, the steel finial of the overhead fixture aimed at him, Doctor Markham decided to cancel his subscription, but with nothing to write with or on, he knew he would forget, and annoyed, he rocked himself out of bed to find a pen and paper.

He did not want to wake Mrs. Railsbeck. Hands out before him, he navigated the upstairs hall, the bump of the runner under one slipper. He found the corner at the top of the stairs and, counting the vinyl treads, creaked down to the living room. Mrs. Railsbeck had vacuumed, and though it hadn't meant a thing at the time, the doctor remembered she had forgotten to slide the ottoman back against his chair. It wasn't in his way, but to prove a point he snuck toward it, taking baby steps, until it met his shin. The doctor sat down. The house was black, dark as the night beyond the porch, starless. In the garage, his Imperial sat half-blinded beside the Rabbit, and all through the crosshatched streets of Tindalls Corners and out into the countryside, darker, maybe snow moving in from the lake, those he had ministered to slept, young and old, some no more, in St. Leo's or Grace Church Cemetery, among family, in other towns alone, following work or love or, in Utica or Syracuse, Buffalo or New York City, dreams. Lives, lifetimes. The doctor sat for a second on the ottoman, his bathrobe falling open, legs chilly, and wondered if he should have become a doctor, if he should have married and lost his wife, if his daughter was happy or like her father, confused but willing. He wondered if Mrs. Railsbeck had expected more of him and if Reynard Vaught knew he forgave him, and after a bit he remembered that he had to go to work tomorrow, and in the dark, treading light and sure as a man on a high wire, he climbed upstairs and into bed.

He woke to the light of snow. He could never get back before nightfall; he was stuck with the Rabbit. Getting breakfast, Mrs. Railsbeck knocked a handful of yellow tabs off the fridge and said, "I knew someone was going to do that."

The county trucks had been out, but Doctor Markham held the Rabbit back. For its box of a shell it was surprisingly quick. Hugging the hilly curves above the junkyard, he thought of his Imperial, how if he did retire, they would need only one car. The Rabbit was a fine car but it was small. It was somehow not them while the Imperial was. But to sell the newer car to fix up the old made no sense.

It was all speculation. He was not going to quit.

He fell asleep after half a sandwich. The goddamn papers. Why did they always keep the heat on high? The windows weren't designed to open. As he slogged his way through December and then January, his head grew thicker. He began to sweat, long, cold strings down his ribs. He kept thinking he had the flu, or his sinuses, a head cold, nothing serious. He knew who he was, where he was. He had eaten lunch. Yet none of the names he was transcribing was familiar.

In his office, he made it through the day, protected by the paperwork. It did not hit him all at once, the way it had before. He even remembered Scott's name to say good-night to him.

It was dark, the parking lot gleaming and vague under the high lights. He could not remember where he had parked his car. He checked his jacket pocket. "Lock Office," one index card read, "Sat Light Odom," another. He walked down one row and up the next, searching for the friendly bulk of the Imperial. Other staff were leaving. Could someone have stolen it? Or towed, they were always towing around the college. It was a hard car to miss, even at night in a large lot. A line had formed at the exit booths, red snow falling through the taillights and exhaust. Panicked, he went back inside to his office and waited.

An hour later the lot was practically empty, the few cars snow-covered, none large enough to be the Imperial. The doctor stood outside the clinic's front doors, looking at his keys. The car key was for a Volkswagen.

"Interesting," the doctor said.

The Volkswagen was, of those left, nearest the doors. The doctor got in and, after stowing his briefcase in back, cranked the motor over, buckled his seatbelt and headed slowly across the lot. At the booth he paid the stranger who knew him and the striped gate rose. The exit emptied onto a side street. Snow had half-hidden the last tracks. He came to a red light. He could go right or left or straight ahead. The light changed. The light changed. The light changed.

The Legion of Superheroes

Larsen did not give up on God till well after the divorce, and by then he was seriously collecting comic books. His son Dylan had turned him on to them before he and Carrie broke up. Saturdays they would drive out over the Highland Park Bridge to Etna and spend a few hours at the Pulp Mill, a dusty-windowed storefront crammed with piles of coverless, yellowing treasures.

In the beginning, Larsen only tolerated his son's interest, chatting with the owner while Dylan and his friend Roger burrowed through the overflowing stacks. It was still a cheap date then, and after a week of battling Carrie, it was a relief, a soft spot, reliable, gratefully awaited. He and the owner, Ned, watched part of the Pitt game on a tiny portable on the counter in back, once in a while split a tallboy in Flintstone jelly glasses. The place was always freezing and breathed the mildewy garage odor of cat. An overstuffed recliner leaned against the back wall, to one side of it a rickety space heater. Larsen sat, filtering Ned's gibberish about the Silver Surfer and the House of Mystery, thinking of how Carrie had said—straight-faced, as if he were the insane one—that she would ask the Assembly to pray for him.

"Go ahead," he said, knowing it would not work. When Larsen prayed now—for it was a habit impossible to stop—halfway through he quit in disgust, as if trying a number he knew full well had been disconnected. In the Assembly you counted only the years since you'd made the change. His new life had lasted fifteen years. Now he was one again, newborn. Every day he thought about going back, but like the memory of his mother, that world and that life seemed to recede into the heavens while he watched,

111

earthbound. It was strange, he thought, that he would miss something he did not want to remember.

Ned kept his new arrivals unpriced on a trunk beside the recliner, and out of boredom or desperation once in a while Larsen leafed through them. He remembered some of the older titles — "Action," "The Flash," "Tales from the Crypt"—and thought them superior to the new ones. They were supposed to be an investment. Why not, he thought.

"'Superman,'" Dylan said, appraising the cover through the plastic protector. "Good choice, Dad; very practical."

He went to the library for price catalogues, every Saturday talked shop with Ned.

"How much?" Carrie would ask before they even had a chance to unpack.

At first Larsen would tell her straight out. After a few months he began to hedge, then outright lie. The last year he'd say, "Don't you worry about it." By then Dylan no longer came in with him, just gave him his bag and ran off to play softball or street hockey until it was safe to slip in the back.

Now Saturday was officially Larsen's day with Dylan. The Pulp Mill was a beer can collectors' store, Roger had moved with his grandmother to Florida, and Larsen's marriage was ugly history. He had left the Assembly while Carrie had plunged further into it, and alone began to feel the dizzying emptiness of being without family. Only his mother's death, long forgotten, safely buried those faithful years, kept him company.

A month ago, despondent after talking on the phone with Dylan, Larsen had tried to kill himself. It was his birthday. He'd bought a day-old cake at the supermarket and topped it with a candle in the shape of the number one. He decorated the top and then the sides with Xanax, pushing the pills into the icing. He opened a quart of milk and sat down and ate the whole thing.

It was foolish, a mistake he realized immediately, whipping the empty vial across the kitchenette. He careened through the apartment to the phone.

"I didn't mean to," he told the operator. "I don't know what I'm doing anymore."

"Nearest cross street?" she said.

The police had called Carrie. She was helpful, if pitiless. Since the attempt, he hadn't seen Dylan.

This Saturday, Larsen was looking for the "Legion of Superheroes" #247, with the origin of the X-Men. The issue would complete his run, and he was prepared to lay out twenty dollars for it. The market was soft; he was hoping to find it cheap at the weekend show out at the Monroeville Sheraton. Driving over, he thought that if he was lucky enough to find a copy, he'd pay whatever the dealer asked. He was early, and stopped at the Rite-Aid for a coffee to waste time.

Carrie let him in. She was made-up, in a skirt and blouse that made him regret his jeans. She punished him with silence. It was foolish, he thought.

"How are things?" he asked. "You look good."

"I'll get him," she said, and went upstairs. He stood in the front hall with his coat zipped to the neck. The new antidepressants gave him the chills. The house hadn't changed, the walls, nothing. A slight vertigo always hit him here, as if he'd been gone for years. He was still paying the mortgage, though Carrie was working full time now at Pitt.

She hadn't looked good, it was just something to say. If the house felt strange in its familiarity, his wife seemed a stranger, unknown and unknowable — as if possessed. It had not been a case, as Larsen first thought, of him and Carrie drifting apart, but the sudden realization on his part that he was living with a crazy woman. Not that he hadn't been taken by religion — and its absence — at times in his life. His mother, before she killed herself, was a devout Lutheran who throughout the sixties clung to her faith like a weapon. A believer, he never blamed God for her death, rather asked his forgiveness, prayed he would not end up the same way. It ran in the family. The Assembly was all he had until he met Carrie. Jesus freaks, her family called them, but as the years and jobs came and went, Larsen's relationship with God grew more comfortable, like a favorite chair. The first signs of the problem seemed tricks of his imagination. How long had Carrie been answering him in parables? Did she ever compare her under-lined bibles, or just shelve one and start another? He began to spy on her, to go through her things, and the more he found the odder she seemed. Yet he knew he had once been that way. He just could not imagine it.

Carrie said it was natural to waver, that from doubt grew faith; despair, hope. But Larsen was not in doubt, and despair was still a good ways off. He felt he had just woken up. She thought he was going mad. They liked to fight in the kitchen, the winner hold-ing their ground, the loser stomping upstairs or, in the rare bout of true rage, out the back door. Sometimes, faced with the night, the sky glowing demonically over the Homestead Works, Larsen would slam the flimsy door of their new Nova and screech down the street for the neighbors to hear (which, ashamed of his own boldness, he immediately regretted), ending up parked on a nearby street, sucking a Slurpee dry, envisioning himself alone in an unfurnished apartment. Until one day it had come to that. Still, that first night among his boxes, the bare walls had surprised him.

Dylan came down ready to go. He had on a Steeler jacket with cracked leather arms, his hands jammed in the pockets. He was a small fourteen, and recently he'd become sullen. October, Car-rie said she'd smelled smoke in his hair. When Larsen asked him, Dylan denied it, but halfheartedly, as if he didn't care what he believed — or worse, as if Larsen wasn't really interested. Larsen trusted it was typical, feared it was personal.

Dylan escaped to the porch.

"Please be back by four," Carrie said.

"Dinner somewhere?" Larsen asked.

"No."

"I'll have him back."

She closed the door behind him. Dylan was waiting by the Nova. It looked like it might snow, might not.

Larsen kept the radio on so they wouldn't have to talk. The Pitt game murmured. Dylan slouched against the door, his hair fogging the window.

"So what's up?" Larsen asked at a light.

"Everything. Mom."

"Yeah?"

"She's going out with this guy tonight."

"Really. How about you?"

"I'm going over to Jimmy's. His mom's going to rent some Nintendo. Pretty basic."

"Who's this guy?"

"Someone from Pitt, I don't know. They're going some nice place over Mount Washington, one of those places with the view."

"Must be rich," Larsen asked.

"He's like a professor, I think. Mom's in this bible group with him. She's always talking about him saying this and that and isn't that interesting and stuff. He's not too bad, I guess. I don't know." They were going through Squirrel Hill, past the kosher meat markets and sooty old newsstands. "So what's the plan, the Sheraton?"

"It's up to you," Larsen said.

"What else is there to do?"

"I don't know, use your imagination."

"No," his son said, "let's just go to the Sheraton."

Larsen swung onto the Parkway East, onto 22 with the mall traffic. It was the way he took to work in the morning, against the rush hour. He was installing boxes for Allegheny Cable. It was boring and paid well. He drifted through other people's homes, ignored, invisible. The company gave him a portable phone so that when the box was all hooked up he could call in and have them activate everything. Every Friday he was going to quit; he was surprised he hadn't yet.

"Dad?" Dylan said. "Mom told me not to tell you about the guy."

"I might get jealous."

"Yeah."

"It's fine. I think it's good. Your mother needs something like that. What do you think?"

"Sure," Dylan said. "I mean, you're OK now."

"I am," Larsen said, and looked over to show him it was true. The boy didn't seem convinced. "What has your mother told you?"

"Nothing. That you were sick."

"I was."

"Like in the head sick."

"That's debatable," Larsen said, but only he laughed.

"She's always saying stuff like that. I just forget it."

"In this case she was telling the truth. Or I don't know, what did she say?"

"She said you took a bunch of pills."

"I did," Larsen said. An identical white Nova passed going the other way. "I was very confused about a lot of things."

"It wasn't because I forgot your birthday."

"Did your mother tell you it was?"

"No. I just remembered after and thought—I don't know, you know."

"It was a lot of things. I really should be able to explain it, shouldn't I?" The boy was looking at him, unsure. "You don't really want to go to the comic book thing."

"Not really."

"How about lunch then? We'll go somewhere you want."

"OK," Dylan said, seeming pleased. "How about Beefsteak Charlie's, they have all-you-can-eat ribs."

"Good," Larsen said, "I like ribs."

The restaurant was part of a chain. It was done in a hokey turn-of-the-century motif, the wallpaper a sepia collage of elevated trains and patent medicine ads, ten-point headlines over illegible type. The host wore a red-and-white striped shirt under a vest and a fake handlebar mustache.

"Nonsmoking," Larsen said.

The menu matched the walls. Larsen ordered the ribs and a beer; Dylan looked at him hopefully.

"Next year," Larsen said.

They drank their ice water and talked about the Steelers and Dylan's school. Larsen always marveled at how his own mother hid in his son's face, and for a few seconds he was so much in love he didn't hear what Dylan was saying. She had used their car, duct-taped the garden hose to the pipe, and pinched it in the window. The day guard found it on the top floor of the parking garage, facing dawn, the tank empty. A gray woman in a hand-knit sweater, buckled upright. Why did he think he could have saved her?

Muzak dixieland and the clank of silverware returned. Dylan was saying something about a girl. Larsen wanted to reach across the table and hold him and tell him he was the only reason he had not laid down in the kitchenette and died, that in that instant when the pills were a knife in his stomach, he had stopped and thought of a moment just like this that he would never see. It was a lie, and the beer coming saved him.

The ribs were fatty, the sauce bland, and the coleslaw came in a pleated paper cup.

"There was this guy at school," Dylan said, and tore off a bite. "Mr. Whaley, our health teacher. He fell in love with this girl in our class named Megan Saunders, and the police arrested him trying to jump off the Panther Hollow Bridge."

"I read about that."

"He was a jerk so it didn't really matter." He stopped in mid-chew, as if he'd bit his tongue.

"I understand," Larsen said.

"I didn't mean it to sound mean."

"That's all right. Another rack?"

"Sure," his son said.

Larsen had a second beer and would have had another if he weren't with Dylan. They sat stuffed, groaning over the bones.

"Is this better than the Sheraton?" Larsen asked.

"I guess. I'm not that into comics anymore."

"I noticed."

"I was thinking I might sell my collection."

Larsen reached for his mug but it was dry. Their waiter had disappeared, probably in back having a smoke. "I'd wait. Prices are down right now." Dylan half-turned away, not listening, and Larsen suddenly felt stupid for pinning his hopes on something so flimsy. "If you need help, I can give you an appraisal. I might even be interested in it myself."

"Can you come over next week?"

"Pick a night," Larsen said. "As long as you clear it with your mother."

"How much do you think I can get for it?"

Not as much as it's worth, Larsen thought, but answered, "I don't know, a lot."

On the way home, Larsen realized it had been snowing since they left the lot. He could not remember turning his wipers on. Pitt was losing big; Dylan fiddled with the knob.

Carrie was surprised to see them back so early. Dylan took him up to his room to have a quick look at the collection. The room had changed, the paint, the light fixture. A gray metal desk he had never seen took up one corner, above it, instead of the Human Torch, a poster of a white Lamborghini. Dylan was pulling out rare issues he had priced from a guide—"Fantastic Four" #1, "Doctor Strange" #1, "Daredevil" #1—all of which Larsen had helped buy, Saturday after Saturday.

"We'll have to put a list together," he said.

"I've got one," Dylan said, and pulled it out of the desk. The prices were current, the total more than Larsen was worth. All his son wanted, it seemed, was his permission.

"I'll check these against what people are actually paying," he said, as if doubtful, and folded the list into a pocket. They stumbled through their good-bye.

Downstairs, as he was tugging on his gloves, Carrie asked if Dylan had asked about what had happened. She only mentioned it because he'd asked her and she'd had to sit down with him.

"I was honest with him," Larsen said, not knowing what it meant. "Have a nice dinner."

"I will," she said.

He drove out to the Sheraton, and after searching until his eyes hurt, found a good (not very good but better than fair, the cover in one piece) copy of the "Legion of Superheroes" #247. He paid the woman fifteen dollars, and with the five he saved bought dinner at a Wendy's. He recognized the girl at the drive-in window; on the way home, he promised himself he would do some real food shopping tomorrow.

He ate his sour burger in silence, then washed and dried his hands before slipping the comic into its plastic cover and taping it shut. He slid it into the bookshelf and stood back to marvel at the complete run. Outside, a car screeched, jerking him upright, but there was no impact. Plastic covers. Was this something to give his life to?

He remembered waking up on the floor, unaware that it was a tube down his throat choking him, that the hand smothering him held an oxygen mask. A white form glowed over him, and all he knew was that he was tired, that he was ready, even if he didn't believe, to go with this angel.

He took out his son's list, unfolded it on the table, and began going through it with a red pen, seeing realistically what he could afford.

Steak

Sheila ignored the two tens on the table in front of her. She did not want steak, and John's insistence on buying dinner for his parents annoyed her. For John the meal was symbolic; for her it was another errand in a day filled with housework.

Sheila turned her back to the bills and watched her mother-in-law, Mrs. Wystrzemski, dry the breakfast dishes. Across the table, Mrs. Zapala, a neighbor Sheila had met only once, gossiped about the new parish priest.

Mrs. Wystrzemski noticed that Sheila avoided touching the money. The girl was proud, she thought; it was acceptable at such a young age.

Sheila swirled another spoonful of sugar into her coffee. John was out looking for work, Becky was upstairs napping, and the morning was settling into a gray calm. She wanted to get back from the store before Becky woke up, but with Mrs. Wystrzemski along it would be impossible. Twice Sheila had offered to return the spoiled sole, and both times John's mother had implied that only someone more experienced could deal with the grocer.

"Father Krooss is old-fashioned," John's mother said, opening the cupboard below the sink. Her hair fell to one side, mud-colored against her black shift. "Old-fashioned is good. They say this new one is an organizer type. He has ideas what a church is for. I say, what, a church? It's a church."

Mrs. Zapala nodded and light flashed from her bifocals. "True. My Stefan says you go to church to pray, not to think." She looked to Sheila, as if for support.

"I'm sure the new one will do fine," Sheila said.

Mrs. Wystrzemski did not want to argue with Sheila again this morning, but with Mrs. Zapala in the room she felt obligated. "I don't like all these new ideas, they get everyone angry. It's better to be happy. Look at the young people, where do the young people go, church? No. Are they happy? No." She waved a skillet, her lips pursed as if about to spit, but the girl was not looking.

Mrs. Zapala dismissed the issue, shooing it with the back of her hand. "They don't care. All they think about is fancy things. Cars, clothes, things like that. Not that they work for them, understand. You see the young people work?"

"What do I know?" John's mother asked. "They go away, they don't stay anymore."

Sheila picked up a grain of sugar by pressing her finger against the table and flicked it away invisibly. The two tens waited for her. It was the first money John had made since they moved back to Pittsburgh. Yesterday he had come home powdered with soot, his good office shoes scuffed, and after changing his shirt had presented her with the two bills. He did not say what he had done, merely handed her the money and said, "This is for steak for everybody tomorrow. It's a tradition, every Wednesday. I'll tell Ma it's a surprise, so don't say anything around Steve or Pops."

Sheila had not argued. Baked potato, broccoli with béarnaise sauce, burgundy. No, they would have beer, and cheese sauce would do. At her parents' house they would insist on a more risqué potato, but while she was at the Wystrzemski's she was expected to act like a daughter, a cook's dim-witted assistant. It was stupid, but she would do it. John had mailed his résumés two weeks ago, and the companies would respond soon. If he felt guilty and wanted to pay their way by buying dinner, fine, she would do it; but only once. In a few months they would be in California or Seattle or Florida, and twenty dollars would seem like nothing again.

Before going to bed, she placed the money on the windowsill so she would not forget. Earlier that morning, while struggling with the sides of Becky's crib, she had noticed it below the snow-framed view of the mills and the river, and remembered. Now the two tens lay before her, nagging as a single sock.

John's mother continued, "People run around crazy today. One day this, one day that. I stop looking at the paper every day. I don't want to know."

Sheila drained her cup. "The world is the same as it always was," she said. "The only difference now is the media. Now you know what's happening around the world. Before you didn't hear about the floods in Turkey, only Johnstown. If there was a war in Africa, you didn't see it on the news so you thought Africa was fine. That didn't mean there wasn't a war there, you just didn't know about it."

"Thank you but I don't want to know," John's mother said, buffing a mug.

"Like she says," Mrs. Zapala agreed, "no one wants these things on their mind. Why should they have to?"

Sheila went to the sink and rinsed out her cup. Outside, behind the frosted window, snow fell lazily, dusting a bare spot in the neighbors' driveway. Through the water, she could hear Mrs. Zapala going on about her son's computer night school and how it would get him a job. She took the tea towel from John's mother, who was following the story with absolute attention. After a long string of words, Mrs. Zapala asked, "Am I right or am I right?"

"We should get going," Sheila said, handing the towel back to John's mother. "They said three-to-six inches this afternoon."

"My knee said snow last night," John's mother said, holding her thigh.

"Signs always," Mrs. Zapala said. She rose from her chair as if in pain, clasping the corners of her fringed shawl together. "No one tells you, you just know. That's what life is."

Sheila tucked the money into the pouch of her purple sweatshirt. "Ready," she prompted. She took her beige coat from the pegboard beside the door, revealing beneath a laminated plaque with the slogan "One day at a time." There were similar plaques nailed to the pine paneling throughout the house, and each time Sheila noticed one, her head gave a jerk, reared back as if struck.

Mrs. Wystrzemski had seen the girl twitch before, and thought it a nervous tic. The older woman attributed it to too much thinking. She tucked her hair inside her collar, knotted her lime babushka under her chin, and pulled on her black trench coat. "All right," she said, stuffing the foil-wrapped sole into her purse.

"If Becky wakes up, don't give her a bottle," Sheila instructed Mrs. Zapala, holding the door open. A few snowflakes crept onto the linoleum. "She shouldn't have anything until noon."

Cars fishtailed up the hill, rears swinging. From the top of McClure Street, Sheila could see the black hull of the Homestead Works, and across the slow, brown Mon, a newer plant, blue with the U.S. Steel trademark painted on the roof. She was going to point out that there was no smoke coming from the stacks and what that meant to the Pittsburgh economy, but John's mother, afraid of falling, was bent over her boots, lagging, oblivious. Sheila stopped at the corner of 21st Avenue and waited for her. Down the street, a group of men huddled around a smoking trash barrel. In front of brick row houses, For Sale signs creaked in the wind.

On Long Island she and John had lost their house. One afternoon he had come home drunk and announced that Grumman had laid him off. He slouched in a chair and wept while Sheila held him.

She was not working at the time, but as soon as she found daycare for Becky, she went back to her job as a foster child caseworker. John took two jobs to meet the mortgage payments, but it wasn't enough, and whenever Sheila suggested that her parents could help, he said, "We'll do it ourselves," and refused to discuss it further.

On a starless December night, a collection agent repossessed their car. John was working the second shift at a self-serve gas station, and every night Sheila picked him up at eleven. Home alone, she was in the living room, trying to feed Becky strained peas, when she heard the crunch of gravel in the driveway. She thought it was someone turning around. The rest of the evening she read, then at 10:30 bundled Becky into her coat, found her keys and license, and clicked on the front porch light. The car was gone. "Perfect," she said.

Even when the policeman delivered the foreclosure papers, Sheila thought they could make it on Long Island. She told her parents it was only temporary, that with a little help they'd brave the hard times. The families she dealt with at work were in much worse shape. But John would not take money from her parents, and so they had moved back to Homestead, planning to stay until John found another engineering job.

Looking at the For Sale signs, Sheila wondered if Father Krooss did anything for the unemployed. She imagined a rumpled man with a hearing aid and dandruff who folded his hands and flexed his fingers when he spoke. He would hold Latin masses and demand proper attire.

Arms stretched out on both sides, purse jiggling on its strap, John's mother tottered toward Sheila like a child learning to roller skate. Though it was fifteen degrees and windy, her legs were bare. In the five years Sheila had known her, she had never once worn pants. Sheila had mentioned it to John, who said, "A dress is as American as she'll go. Women don't wear pants in the old country." She reminded him that this was the new country. "She can kneel faster in a dress," John had replied. Sheila remembered this and smiled, picturing his mother on her knees in the snow, praying for a new, mindless daughter-in-law.

Mrs. Wystrzemski grabbed the stop sign with both hands, her purse circling the pole until it ran out of strap, then unwinding. The girl turned and started to cross without her. "Slow down please, Sheila."

The girl stopped, came back, and took her by the arm. They moved together toward the curb.

"Slow, slow," Mrs. Wystrzemski urged. At the corner, she noticed the men around the barrel. One of them wore a leather jacket, another had long blond hair and a mustache. She switched her purse to her other shoulder. "Careful with these," she whispered.

"There's nothing wrong with those men. They don't have jobs so immediately people think they're trouble." The girl let go of her hand.

"So they should get a job," Mrs. Wystrzemski said, taking hold of the girl's wrist. Steadied, she looked up and saw the blonde one spit in the fire, and as he leaned back, she saw a beer can.

"There aren't any jobs here," Sheila explained, her free hand gesturing to the mills far below. "John can't find a job. How are these men supposed to? Is anyone helping them?"

"Papa has a job. It's the young ones who don't want to work hard." A salt-rotted Chevy passed, and they crossed the street. "They should go get a job," John's mother said, clinging to Sheila's arm as they neared the opposite curb. "And clean up and get a hair cut and not be drinking all the time on the sidewalk."

"And be nice boys and go to church," Sheila added.

"Maybe if they went before this wouldn't happen."

Sheila laughed. "Maybe they should have been priests! Priests never lose their jobs!" John's mother said nothing, but half a block from the men, Sheila felt her tugging toward the street. Sheila dug in and pulled her to the center of the sidewalk. "Stop treating them like criminals. Think how they must feel."

Mrs. Wystrzemski was silent. The girl was walking slower now, and as they approached the men, she veered toward them. Mrs. Wystrzemski's purse slid from her shoulder and hung on her arm, swung between them, but the girl did not seem to notice. The man in the leather jacket turned his head. His dark hair was slicked back, a greasy lock dangling above his eyes. Mrs. Wystrzemski reached across her body and restored her purse to her shoulder. In the ring of men snow flew upward from the flames.

Fire licked through quarter-sized holes in the barrel, leaving black spikes and streaks on the rusted metal. The girl stopped and asked, "How's it going?"

The man with the greasy hair dropped his can of Iron City into the barrel, and a shower of sparks leapt up behind him and died in the air. His eyes played over the girl's shape. "Hey, you know," he mumbled, "things are great." A cigarette burned in his hand.

The girl stepped toward him, and Mrs. Wystrzemski's hand dropped from her arm. "My husband's looking for work," the girl said. "Do you know if U.S. Steel's hiring?"

The man blew a stream of smoke. "Forget them, they're down the tubes." He glanced at Mrs. Wystrzemski. His face seemed familiar to her; not one of John's friends, though. She could not connect his eyes with those of any neighborhood child, yet as he spoke she recognized him, and he, with a leer, seemed to acknowledge this. After each sentence he smiled, the ends of his lips drawn up into his cheeks, as if any second he would begin to laugh and call the girl a fool. Mrs. Wystrzemski took a firm step and clutched the girl's arm. The man went on, "There's American Bridge but you got to be what they call skilled."

The girl ignored Mrs. Wystrzemski's grip. "So you've been looking for a long time."

"You're damned right," the man said, then to Mrs. Wystrzemski added, "excuse me, ma'am." The sprig of hair touched the blank space between his eyebrows.

"We are late," Mrs. Wystrzemski interrupted. "We have to go." She sank her heels into the snow and yanked the girl away.

Sheila caught herself and tried to stop, but John's mother was dragging her downhill. She turned her head and saw the man give John's mother the finger. "What is wrong with you?" she asked.

"Bad men." The old woman bulled forward in the snow, one hand holding the knot of her babushka.

"They don't have jobs so they're automatically bad people, right? He's probably been looking all over the valley, just like John.

But you wouldn't understand that. You don't know what it means to be looked down on by people simply because they have money and you don't."

"Bad men, you talk to bad men. Drinking, dirty, long hair."

"What are you talking about? You drink beer, you have long hair." Sheila had regained her lead. Now that they were safely away from the men, the old woman seemed to have lost her strength. She leaned against Sheila as if exhausted, the purse crushed between their hips. Sheila felt in her pocket for the twenty dollars, then remembered it was in her sweatshirt. She held John's mother's arm and steered her down McClure.

The Giant Eagle stood on the corner of Eighth Avenue and McClure, its plate-glass windows covered by plywood sheets. Uneven blue spray paint advertised "Parking in Back." The management had salted both the driveway and sidewalk, and when Sheila stepped onto the bare concrete, her feet slid on the unmelted crystals. At the same instant, John's mother slipped, and only their falling in opposite directions kept them on their feet. Someone laughed loudly in a high-pitched voice.

The laugh had come from a child standing by the electric doors, soliciting the customers as they entered. John's mother brushed Sheila's hand from her arm and advanced on the child. Sheila hurried after her.

He was a short, thin boy. Attached to his back and chest by a belted harness were four metal rods supporting a white plastic helmet which encased his head. His neck, a string of tendon surrounding a prominent windpipe, bulged as he breathed. John's mother stopped short of him, holding her purse to her chest with both hands. Sensing her fear, Sheila stepped between her and the child and patted his shoulder. The child gurgled, shook the change in his can. "When we come out," Sheila said. "Right?" she asked John's mother, but Mrs. Wystrzemski had passed them without looking and disappeared through the electric doors. Sheila tapped the boy's can, winked and followed her in.

Inside, John's mother seemed to have forgotten the child. She stood by a pyramid of soda, jabbering in Polish with a woman who wore a similarly horrible green babushka, a black trench coat buttoned up to her neck, and boots. The old woman would never learn as long as John's father kept his job. Sheila had seen the same blindness in her co-workers at the foster care agency. They told people everything would be fine if they had faith and worked hard. John's mother used the same criteria, but negatively. People's misfortunes were a product of lack of faith and laziness; success was inexplicable.

There were only two checkout lines open, and the first aisle, the fruits and vegetables, was empty. Above the shelves plastic covers of fluorescent lights hung down like trapdoors. Sheila chose a basket, unbuttoned her coat, and took the twenty dollars from the pouch of her sweatshirt. She noticed there were no artichokes, no brussels sprouts. The few cucumbers were spotted with wet wounds. Sheila looked down the aisle, hoping to call John's mother over and point out the condition of the store, but both old women were gone.

She saw them again while searching through the meat rack. They stood in the middle of the bread aisle, carrying on their conversation, hands fluttering. There were gaps on the shelves beside them where the management must have deleted items to save money. Sheila watched them for a second, then turned back to the meat.

Early shoppers had bought all the hamburger, but there were plenty of steaks. On Long Island, Sheila had gone to a butcher, and the cuts she inspected now seemed fattier, white tributaries invading the red flesh. She poked her thumb into the cellophane to feel for bones, discarded package after package.

While she was sorting out the five best, standing back from the cooler, imagining how much better her dinner would be than the bland stews and roasts John's mother served, the handicapped child appeared around the corner. He moved jerkily, one shoulder twisted behind, as if someone were holding him back. His helmet, attached to his angled torso, forced his face to the right, so that only one of his bug-eyes was visible to her. As he neared, he rattled his can.

John's mother and her twin were still gabbing away in the bread aisle. "Come on," Sheila whispered to the child, now jangling the coins at her. She tapped the top of the can and pointed to the two old women. Careful of his harness, she gently pushed him away from her and up the aisle.

He dragged himself toward the women, swaying between the half-empty shelves. John's mother did not seem to notice him, but the other woman turned her head and kept it locked on the child. Sheila ducked behind a tower of sugar wafers. Frozen, the other woman stared at the boy, and soon John's mother stopped talking and turned to see what she was looking at. The child raised the can above his helmet, pushing it first at the other woman, then at John's mother. As if being robbed, she dug through her purse, tissues and pens falling to the floor, her head down, avoiding the child. She reached her hand to the can and dropped in a coin, then took the other woman by the arm and hustled her away.

When Sheila came around the dairy aisle and into the check-out area, John's mother was nowhere in sight. The child aimlessly waved his can at a cardboard cutout of a TV chef. Sheila joined the shorter line, behind a white-haired man in a VFW wind-breaker with American flags on its sleeves. She lifted the basket onto the end of the belt and waited for the old man to push his dog food forward.

The cashier, a thick-jowled woman with crooked teeth and an ill-fitting red wig, rang up Sheila's purchases. Sheila had the twenty dollars out, ready for the total. The woman punched the register with the heel of her hand, popped open the cash drawer, and said, "Twenny thirty-three."

Sheila gave her the two tens and began to bag the vegetables.

"Scuse me," the cashier said, chewing gum. "Need thirty-three more cents."

Sheila went through her pockets. "I'll bring it tomorrow."

"Can't do it," the woman said, the two tens flat on her palm. "Been happening too much lately. If it was up to me, honey, I'd say sure, but my manager says cash in full."

"I don't have it."

"Then just take something back." She tore the receipt from the register and began running the next customer's purchases through the electronic scanner.

Sheila grabbed one of the steaks — her steak, a steak she didn't even want — and shook it at the cashier. "Thirty-three fucking cents!" she screamed, and pushed through the line. The other customers stepped aside. Steaming for the bread aisle, she heard a dry female voice say, "Man must be out of work."

She stopped, turned and faced the line. "You see what this is?" she yelled. "Steak. Understand? Steak."

She threw the steak into the bin, then, furious, snatched it back out and jammed it into the waist of her jeans and pulled her sweatshirt over it. It was cold against her stomach. Someone laughed, and her gaze shot to the mirrors above the meat. The handicapped child stood behind her, rattling his can, grimacing vacantly. She laughed back at his reflection. She smoothed her front, motioning the child to follow her, and walked up the bread aisle.

Before turning into the checkout area, she scrunched up her face and practiced a snarl. The cellophane pinched her skin. As Sheila rounded the corner, face set, the cashier spotted her and waved. The line parted and Sheila drove through to the register. "Satisfied?" she asked.

The cashier handed her the reciept, counted out the bills one by one onto her palm and placed the change on top of them. "Sorry," she said, "I don't make the rules around here."

"I know, you just follow them blindly." She dropped the receipt and the money into the bag. "Thanks a lot," Sheila called so the line could hear her. "Have a nice day!" She headed for the door, holding the bag tightly against her stomach.

The handicapped child was cutting through an empty lane in front of her. She stopped and fished through the bag for some change, balancing it on one raised knee. The steak rode up and poked her in the stomach, but she was far enough from the cashier to feel safe. She found a quarter and a nickel, hefted the bag and wrapped both arms around it.

The child's hand tossed from side to side, and with her arms around the bag, Sheila could not hit the slot in the top of the can. A styrofoam corner of the package stuck out from her sweatshirt. "Let's go," she said, walking away from him. "Come on, I'll give it to you outside."

The automatic door swept open when she stepped on the mat. Outside, against the storefront, John's mother sat on a bench, still talking with the other woman. Sheila hugged the bag to her stomach. Behind her, the child mumbled loudly, garbled nonsense. The second door swept open, and Sheila stepped out into the cold.

As she stepped off the mat, the child plowed into her from behind, knocking her forward. Her shoes slipped on the salt and she began to fall. She threw her arms out for balance, and the bag flew. On her way down, twisting, she reached for the child, her hand hitting the can, swatting it away from him, and as her head met the pavement, coins showered around her.

The vegetables lay in the salt, ruined. Her hands burned, and she felt snow melting on her skin. She brought her hand to her stomach to hide the steak, a quarter peeling away from the scraped flesh of her palm, but by that time John's mother was standing above her, looking down at her as if peering over the edge of a cliff. At her feet sat the steak, its wrapper torn.

After helping Sheila and the child up, John's mother gathered the groceries and fit them back in the bag. The steak rested on top. Dazed, Sheila sat on the bench and held her head. The other woman patted her arm, soothing her with gibberish.

Mrs. Wystrzemski knelt and scooped the coins and salt in a pile and filled the crushed can. The child stood motionless beside her, as if lost. She found the lid, closed it and handed the can to the boy. She made sure his contraption was on straight, then asked the girl, "You are all right?"

She nodded. Her hands were bleeding. There were traces of red in her hair.

"I'll carry," Mrs. Wystrzemski said, and picked up the bag. The boy dragged himself back to his station by the doors.

They crossed from the bare patch onto the snow, arm-in-arm. Sheila's hands stung, and she did not want to bloody John's mother's coat. They turned up McClure and slowly climbed the hill, silent. The men at the barrel were gone, the fire burnt out. Cars swerved and braked, their front tires sliding. The For Sale signs swung in the wind.

At the top of the hill they turned right onto 22nd. As they approached the stairs of John's house, Sheila said, "You saw."

John's mother did not answer.

"You saw it."

"What do I see?" John's mother said. "It is nothing."

Sheila stopped. "Don't pretend," she said angrily. "Say what you want to say."

Mrs. Wystrzemski turned to her. Over the top of the bag she could see only her face. The girl was breathing hard, and under her left eye there was a smear of blood, as if she had been in a fight. "Sheila, you are a good person, you know that. Everything will be fine."

"No, everything will not be fine," the girl shouted. "Everything is fucked-up. Why can't you admit it?" Her mouth stayed open, her breath coming in quick clouds. Mrs. Wystrzemski looked into the bag. The meat was leaking. "It's not my fault," said the girl. "It's not John's either. It's nobody's fault." She waited for confirmation, and when Mrs. Wystrzemski said nothing, the girl ran up the stairs and onto the porch.

Alone, Mrs. Wystrzemski repeated softly, "Everything will be fine."

Mrs. Zapala was watching TV in the living room, picking at a box of chocolates. She told Sheila, "The baby's asleep the whole time."

"Thank you," Sheila mumbled through the hand covering her face, and hurried upstairs, still wearing her coat. Carrying a bag of groceries, Mrs. Wystrzemski came into the room, glanced at Mrs. Zapala and left.

Mrs. Wystrzemski drew three dollar bills out of the wet bag. She put the money on the kitchen table and began tearing the wrapper off the steak. She turned on the cold tap.

Behind her, Mrs. Zapala asked, "So, can she shop?"

"She has a hard time," Mrs. Wystrzemski answered.

"Like everyone."

"No, it is not," Mrs. Wystrzemski said, washing the salt off the meat. Water tinged with blood ran over her hands. "It is not."

The Big Wheel

Crandell never noticed the house before it was on fire. It was in Central Islip in a ratty neighborhood — kids hanging out by salt-rotted cars, cruddy lumps of snow. Crandell was on his way home after holding the O'Neill kid for detention. A smart mouth, asked him if a wood screw felt anything like a real one. Crandell called Millie from the teacher's lounge to say he'd be late.

He wasn't used to such heavy traffic going home, and he was letting it get to him. He shouldn't have let O'Neill get to him. He wasn't a bad kid, just a joker, the kind of kid who'd only started to go the wrong way. Crandell had seen it before and knew the best thing was to let it pass. He had to watch his blood pressure. No point wasting all of that broccoflower, all that turkey pastrami. He was first in line at the light — poised to beat the next — when he noticed in an upstairs window a curtain waving in flames. He made to open his door and the Century stalled; someone behind him honked. He ran across the intersection, pointing at the window. He figured someone would follow.

The house was a duplex, there were two buzzers. A woman in a scorched housecoat stumbled through the door, screaming "My baby! My baby!"

"Where?" he asked, grabbing her wrists as if she might lie.

There wasn't even smoke in the downstairs, but above him the fire was loud. A cloud floated in the second floor, opaque and slow as fog, smelling sharply of plastic. At the top of the stairs his lungs turned to chalk. He dropped to his hands and knees and held his tie over his nose and mouth. Flames poured up the walls.

The baby was not a baby but a girl at least four years old. She was in the first bedroom he looked in, under the bed. She crawled out, and he held her to him and sidestroked the way to the stairs. Bits of burning lath rained through the smoke. He wanted to straighten up to carry her down, but the fire seemed to have moved downstairs, and when he did risk a full step he missed and fell — out of the smoke and onto the girl. She was shrieking; he had hurt her. He lay at the foot of the stairs, stunned. In the foggy room across the hall, curtains were burning. A piano was going up silently, a lamp. He picked the girl up and bulled out the front door.

The woman took her from him and caressed her, shushed her. She thanked and thanked him, all the time soothing the child, who was crying steadily. People had stopped on the sidewalk; one young woman came into the yard and suggested they stand back from the house. The mother bent down to salvage a Big Wheel but couldn't manage it with the child. Crandell picked it up and looked around the yard for anything else worth saving. There was a chain with no dog on it, that was about it.

Sirens were closing on them. The child was whimpering; it was her wrist, already ballooning. He had left the front door of the house open, and skeins of fabric drifted out, glowing, floated across the porch and fell to the dirt. A window cracked and pieces dropped to the tin porch roof. "Check it out," a boy behind him cheered.

The EMT's took the girl first. They were both women, crisp and confident in their uniforms. He took a dizzying drink of oxygen. The mother — Mrs. DeLuca — was telling them how he had saved her little girl.

"We got a hero here," the one EMT told the other.

"Anyone else?" the other said, offering the rubber mask around. Crandell wanted more but thought it might not be good for him; his heart was tripping as it was. He sat on the back bumper with his head between his knees, spitting black, until the EMT's said they were sorry but they had another call. They clunked shut the rear doors and got in and shot away.

The firemen were inside. A different engine was hosing down

the house next door; the gutters streamed. The police had put up orange horses. His car sat in the middle of the fire engines, trapped by hoses. Someone had put a ticket on it. The Big Wheel sat by the curb; he picked it up.

"Hey," someone called. It was the woman who'd told them to stand back. She had a news team with her. "This is him. He went in the house and got her when it was on fire."

"Is that right, sir?" the reporter asked. He had neat hair, and eyeliner. His coat had the NBC peacock sewn over the heart.

"I have to go," Crandell said.

The reporter made him spell his name and told him what questions he would ask when they were on camera. "Don't practice," he said, "just let it come out."

"Can I put this down?" Crandell said about the Big Wheel.

"Can you get it?" the reporter asked the cameraman.

"I'll shoot him long and zoom him."

"Sure," the reporter said, "put it down if you want."

"Beautiful," the cameraman said. Other crews were stacked up waiting for him, shooting the roof, the trucks, the crowd.

The house was a wet wreck when Crandell finished answering, the siding warped and bubbled. The DeLucas wouldn't be coming back here. He hauled the Big Wheel along by one handlebar. The spotlights had given him a headache; the afternoon seemed dim. A pumper sat half on the sidewalk, its crew in the front yard, mopping up. The real rush hour had begun, and people slowed to see what was happening. A reporter had moved his car for him, pledging to take care of the ticket, and he had to search for it. He put the Big Wheel in the back.

He would be late getting home. Millie would have their trays up and Peter Jennings on. His dinner would be in the oven, getting hard—and he was ravenous now, he wanted to take her out for a steak. The car stank of smoke. He sniffed his cuff, his tie. The whole thing hadn't sunk in yet; it would take a while, he supposed.

"I can't believe it," Millie said. "You were on all three newses."

She put a little extra into his kiss and took his things, wincing at the smell of his coat. The phone rang. "I'm going to have to send this out," she said. It rang again. "These people have been calling nonstop, you have no idea."

"Do you want me to get it?"

"They don't want to talk to me."

"It might be George."

"I just talked to Eleanor on Tuesday."

It was the *Post.* He told them to call back tomorrow.

"I had chicken going," she said, "but I figured you'd want to celebrate."

"Let me change," he said, going up.

"Or are you too tired?"

"Just McCluskey's."

"I already called," she said.

He had the New York strip, black and pink with garlic salt and butter gobbed on, a steaming potato with a blob of sour cream and fresh chives, and two Strohs. Couples came by the booth to shake his hand when his mouth was full. The cook came out of the kitchen.

"Now you know how Jackie Kennedy feels," Millie said.

Their waitress told him there was no check.

"I could get used to this," Crandell said, and left her a ten.

"Del," Millie scolded.

"Del nothing," he said.

They stayed up for the news. Millie made popcorn. His face looked fat, and no one had told him about the soot above his lip. His hair seemed thin. He looked awful; he looked dead.

"She came out and said her girl was in there so I went in and got her."

"Were you thinking that your life might be in danger at that point?" the reporter asked.

"I just went in. I knew she was in there and I went in after her. I wasn't really thinking at that point."

It sounded average, and at first he was ashamed, then angry with the reporter for putting him on the spot.

"Look at you," Millie said. "You look like a hero, all that gunk all over your face. I wish we had a video thing to show George and the kids, they'd love this."

"I sound like an idiot."

"You sound fine. You sound like everyone sounds."

A plane crashed in Chile, and he got up and turned.

Onscreen, parts of the DeLuca's roof fell in. "There were no serious injuries," the anchorwoman said, and they segued into the weather.

"That's all folks," he said.

"I'll have to go out and buy some *Newsday*s tomorrow," Millie said. She cuffed some stray popcorn off the cushions and gave him his good-night kiss. "You'll lock up?"

Mornings Crandell kept the radio off in the car. He liked to drive and think. About the Sunday poker game at Reece's or, now that it was December, the next Rangers telecast. Nothing ever happened in his daydreams. They were all quiet and soft light, warmth, sometimes a sandwich. And then he would drop back into the car, like those old Hertz commercials, and see he had missed Bohemia entirely. Where Sunrise opened to four lanes and traffic sped up, he jockeyed off onto the access road and made his morning stop at Martone's Deli.

Today he bought a paper with his coffee. Martone asked him how was tricks.

"You didn't see the paper?" Martone's daughter-in-law said. She was mixing antipasto and had on transparent gloves.

Martone turned a *Newsday* around on the counter. "I don't see anything."

"It's in a little," she said. She couldn't touch the pages and he couldn't find it. "I don't know, but it's him — Mr. Crandell." She told the story.

"Well," Martone said. "Congratulations."

Crandell shrugged as if it wasn't his fault. "Can't be late," he said.

In the lot, getting in, he saw the Big Wheel in the backseat. The interior smelled sour, like wet ash.

He slowed to miss the light by the house but the green was long in the morning. Someone had nailed plywood over the windows and put up notices he couldn't read. He wondered where the De-Lucas were, what kind of insurance they had. Renters probably.

He figured Ward would stroll over from metal shop and give him a hard time about it, and he was right. A few minutes into the paper, he heard a fake squeaky voice go, "Help, help" and turned to the door. A hand with a lit cigarette lighter danced in the frame.

"I'll save you," said a gruff voice, and a second hand snatched the lighter away.

"My hero," the squeaky hand said, and the two hands meshed.

Ward stepped forth. "Del, fifty-nine? Is that right, next stop the big six-oh?"

"Don't believe everything you read," Crandell said, though it was true.

"And what exactly are these misdemeanor charges pending on this DeLuca woman?"

"I haven't gotten that far."

"You picked a winner, Del. It says she's been in and out of jail since she was sixteen. She's one of those people the system gets ahold of and doesn't let go. She just got the kid back."

"Will you let me read it myself?"

"And I told everyone fame wouldn't change you." He patted Crandell on the back.

"Take a leap," Crandell said.

In two weeks the semester would be over; the kids were acting like it already was. The house they were building was pretty much finished. The little Cape seemed huge indoors. It covered the long back wall of the shop, a single face with two windows, a door and a slope of roof. The Pergament on Hempstead Turnpike donated everything. When it was done, Crandell would come in one weekend and tear it down, salvage what he could and send Pergament a list of what he needed for next semester's. He had first period work on shingling, second the roof, while he thought about the DeLucas.

Third was his free period, and he called the fire department. They told him to call the police, who referred him to the Department of Social Services. They gave him the address of the fire.

"If it just happened yesterday, we're not going to have it," the man told him.

"Who *would* have it?"

"We are the only ones that would have it."

"When?" Crandell asked.

"When their caseworker files it. Right now they're probably in some sort of temporary housing."

"Where?"

"The caseworker would have all that information but she's probably out there with them right now."

"When will she be back?"

"I honestly can't tell you," the man said.

"Thank you," Crandell said.

Sixth period, O'Neill came in twenty minutes late, his jean jacket stinking of dope. The rest of the kids were up on the roof, banging away.

"I'm marking you absent," Crandell said. "And you've got detention."

"Don't sweat it, Delbert."

"What is it with you?" The hammering had stopped, the class was watching them. "Go to the office," Crandell said.

O'Neill shrugged and held up his hands to show he was innocent, turned, and walked out the door. The hammering started up again.

In detention, O'Neill was the same kid. It wasn't just show, he really didn't care. It was the dope, Crandell figured. He'd seen him out by the smokestack, getting stoned at seven A.M., or walking by his windows during class time. He wasn't a bad kid—an evil kid the way some were. He liked the lathe. Crandell told him he could leave after a hundred shingles, and stood there to count. The boy put them up crooked, but he knew the steps and his stroke was sure. He took off his jacket.

"So you're supposed to be the big hero," the boy said.

"That's me."

"You saved that girl's life?"

"Yeah."

"That's wild, you."

"It could have been anyone."

"No," the boy said, and stopped. His eyes were pink. "No, it was you. It's like, it was waiting there for you—like you go through all this other bullshit just to do that one thing, you know what I'm saying?"

"Sure."

"Don't believe it."

"I won't," Crandell said.

On his way home, watching the house pass, he glimpsed the Big Wheel behind him. On Sunrise he passed a cop doing seventy-five. They had broiled sole and he wasn't on the news.

"They lost them," he told Millie.

"Who lost who?"

"The people from the fire."

"There are people who get paid to take care of these kinds of situations."

"They're the ones who lost them."

"I'm sure whoever is responsible is doing the best they can."

On the phone, George thought the same. He was more interested in the fire, in how his father felt in the burning house.

"I remember I was surprised when I fell down the stairs. I didn't have time to take inventory."

"You were there," George said.

"Sorry."

They put Craig on but he wouldn't say anything so they put Sherry on. "When you goed in the fire?" she brought out.

"Went."

"When you went in the fire was it scary?"

"Yes," Crandell said.

"Sometimes Craig gets scared of Mighty Mouse and I have to turn off the television."

"Aha. Is Daddy there?"

Eleanor came on and talked about plans for Christmas, then George came on again. Crandell checked the clock; the call was getting expensive. He mentioned it and said he'd remember something about the fire for next Tuesday.

The steak the night before had done something to him. He read in the john and got to bed late. He had to watch it becoming a habit. That was how people got killed driving to work, they'd fall asleep and pancake the person in front of them, shoot across the median.

The next morning he was careful to make his exits. Snowflakes dissolved on the windshield. A stake truck sat in the mud yard of the house, on the tailgate several men in work boots and hard hats sharing coffee and smoking. The Big Wheel was still behind him. He would call DSS again, maybe they'd know something by now.

A few blocks from school he saw O'Neill trudging uphill. The boy had on his jean jacket, his hands jammed in his pants pockets. Crandell slowed beside him and hit the button for the passenger window.

"Want a lift?" he called.

"That's all right."

"Come on, you're getting soaked."

"No, really, Mr. Crandell, go ahead. I got to meet some of my boys."

"See you in class," Crandell said, and pointed, "on time this time."

There was nothing in the paper. Ward came in during homeroom, shaking his head. "Yesterday's heroes," he said, "where are they now?"

First period finished the house. He had second work on their own projects and dug up some pine for anyone who wanted to hone up on the router. No one seemed very enthused. He would have to put something together for the last week of class. He had the crazy idea it was all the work O'Neill did that threw off the schedule. Sitting at his desk with his feet up on the pullout, with the house across from him, complete, over, Crandell thought it might be good to get the kids involved with the teardown. Maybe give O'Neill a thrill, let him claw off the first shingle.

This time the guy at DSS was polite. He gave Crandell an address in Bellport, practically in his own backyard. Millie knew some people over at St. Jude's who might be able to do something for them. It was better than Islip, especially for a kid. Last year a kid in his fourth period got shot over a pair of sunglasses—a kid like O'Neill, just wild enough to be in the wrong place with the wrong crowd. It was way better than Islip, and the news kept him whistling.

The bell starting sixth period rang, and no sign of O'Neill. Crandell lingered in the hall, hopeful, then toed the stop up and closed the door.

"He's here," Mervin Tate said, "I saw him at lunch."

"Thank you for the news," Crandell said.

He let them work on their own stuff.

Halfway through class, a few boys behind him started laughing. O'Neill was passing by outside, waving. Crandell hustled down the hall, around the turn, and bulled through the heavy outside doors, but the kid had taken off. He stood in the meager snow, gasping. His class pressed against the windows.

The stake truck was crammed with lumber. Next to it sat a huge blue dumpster. The workmen had rigged a tube to a second floor window; debris slid into the dumpster and threw up clouds of dust. Someone behind him honked; the light had changed.

He knew the address; it was a quiet street down near the water. Summers he and Millie would cruise through around sunset and watch the gulls and fishermen, the ferry to Fire Island coming back packed with bleary day-trippers. The bungalows had once been summer homes but were now fenced off from each other, big Chevys falling apart in sandy drives. Rushes grew in the ditches, dinghies rotted on the mud flats. Today, with the snow and the wind off the water, the long vistas, it seemed desolate. Crandell searched the mailboxes for numbers.

He was a block away when he saw the motel. It was low, eight or nine units hidden by a shaggy pine hedge. He'd thought it had gone under. The sign was missing its neon, just a big swooped arrow pointing to the drive. He did not have to look at the address.

He pulled up next to the office. As he was getting out, he saw a man peek from behind the curtain of number one, then pull back out of sight.

The office was locked and dark. He went to number one and knocked on the door.

The man who'd been peeking answered; he left the chain on. "Yeah?" he said.

"I'm looking for an Irene DeLuca and her daughter."

"That for the girl," the man said, pointing to the Big Wheel. His teeth didn't fit right and he spoke too loud.

"You know her."

"As much as I care to. Number nine."

The girl answered the door. She had a cast on her wrist. The room behind her was dark, in a corner a TV mutely strobing cartoons. She did not recognize him, but saw the Big Wheel and took it from him. It was too heavy for her and dropped with a clunk. The place was stifling hot and reeked of cigarettes; on the dresser sat a clump of beer cans, red in the cartoon light.

"Is your mother here?" Crandell asked.

"She went out with Manny's friend." She got a coat — brand new but cheap, an ugly orange — pushed the Big Wheel out the door and closed it behind them. She pedaled a few feet, then looked up at Crandell. "Did you bring a bottle?"

"No."

"Someone's going to bring a bottle."

"Someone," Crandell said.

"Someone Manny knows."

She bumped over the curb and started doing a circle, the plastic wheels drumming over grit. A different TV was going somewhere inside. His was the only car in the lot.

"Will you tell your mother that Mr. Crandell from the fire came by?"

The girl finished the circle and stopped next to him. "You're not a fireman," she said. "You don't have a fire hat."

"Tell her Mr. Crandell," he said.

"Crandell, Wandle, Dandle," she said, and started off again. He hustled across the lot to cut her off, but stopped halfway, at the center of the circle. It was snowing again, and the road was empty, the lot quiet except for the Big Wheel. He looked at the ruined sign, the rusty blue Pepsi machine with its thin door, the moss between the shingles. She was still going around when he pulled out.

The next day O'Neill didn't show again. Crandell kept stepping out into the hall, hoping.

"You didn't hear, Mr. C.?" Mervin Tate said.

"Hear what?"

"He's in Juvie. He got picked up over Wyandanch last night."

Crandell broke out the prybars and sledges. He did not try to instruct them, only warned them not to hurt themselves. They buttoned their sleeves and tugged their gloves on. The only things off limits were the door and window frames. He sent them in in shifts, switching every few minutes. At first they were uncertain, but after the first assault they were hacking and slashing, amazed they were allowed. By the end of the period it was all down. They left sweating and happy.

The bells rang, in ten minutes rang again to clear the building. Ward came by with his lunch pail and his *Newsday* and said he'd see him at the game Sunday. "Little early?" he asked about the house.

"A little," said Crandell.

He walked down to the lounge and called Millie, bought a coffee and came back through the empty hall, shoes scuffing on the marble. He pinched off his tie tack, unclipped the tie and dropped it on his desk, then rolled down his sleeves, pulled on a pair of gloves, and began sorting through the wreckage, trying to decide what could and could not be saved.

Econoline

Willie T. saw the van on his way home from the bakery. Fat and rounded, it leaned in Waynoka Ford's used lot, one rusted brake set on a cinder block. "Where's that from?" he asked Gar, slowing. Gar shrugged and kept walking. Willie T. sped up, caught him. "You seen it before?" Gar shook his head. "Nice van to be for sale round here," Willie T. said. "Real nice van."

Gar stopped and faced him. "Now why are you worrying about some van?" he said, pointing to the van with his lunch pail. "You don't got enough trouble without worrying about some dumb van?"

Willie T. looked at him, then away, then at the van. "All I'm saying is, it's a nice van for around here."

"Like you're gonna buy it or something."

"If I have a mind to."

"You don't have to worry about that," Gar said. "That van's five, six thousand easy. Mind to, go on." He started walking.

They walked the refinery fence, stacks black in the dusk, and up onto the bridge. Below, sunk in the mud, a doorless refrigerator gleamed white. Gar said, "Sometimes you're like them Indians. Know they're gonna lose and they go to the movie anyway. Be wishing all the time." A tractor-trailer loaded with steel pipe rumbled by, shaking the bridge. Willie T. watched it around the bend. "What're you gonna do with something like that anyway?" Gar asked.

"I'll haul people around. Like the kids goin' to school. Like the meals-on-wheels. Yeah, and I'll haul around stuff too. Groceries and junk. You can do anything with a van."

"Give me shit, haul people around. The county's got people to do that already. Plus you got to have more than one. Schools got a whole yard full of vans, with special paint jobs and everything."

"I'd fix it up to look good, think I'm stupid? It'd be just as good as them fancy vans. Better, cause I'd look after it too."

"Shit, you're gonna die on Nabisco time like the rest of us. Just getting upset over nothing."

They went by the lit Arco station and over the tracks into town, passed Big Ed's Tavern and the bowling alley and came to Gar's street. "All right, Willie T., I'll see you tomorrow. And don't think them cookies are gonna disappear overnight. They'll be waiting on you in the morning."

"Yeah, they'll be waiting on you too. All right, Gar, tomorrow."

Before dinner, Willie T. told Christine about the van. Boots off, he sat back in his stuffed chair, talking through the open kitchen door. Pans clattered and rang through the apartment. "That's fine," she called from the stove, as if she'd heard him, "That sounds fine, honey." But he knew she hadn't heard him, and he let it go. No sense stirring things up before he had to.

He mentioned it again over the chicken and rice, a quick remark. "Is that what you were yelling at me before?" she asked, and shoveled another forkful.

"It's just nothing," Willie T. said. "What were you up to today?"

In bed that night, Christine snoring in the other twin, he thought about what he could do with the van. He had a few more years at the bakery, two, maybe three, but after that, who knew? His pension and Social Security went only so far. Rent alone would chew up what they had in the bank, and they weren't poor enough for assistance. After he retired he'd have to get some kind of job, he knew that already, and driving around all day seemed like good part-time work. He'd miss Gar and the guys, but if there were passengers he'd talk to them. Maybe there'd be kids, that would be great. Or deliveries, and that would be OK too, as long as he didn't have to load and unload. He lay in the darkness, listening to Christine, imagining himself at the wheel, a hack's cap pulled down over his forehead. The windows were clean and the sun shone, rays bright streaks along the polished metal. In the windshield reflections of overhanging trees rose like flocks of wild birds.

When they went by it, twice a day, to and from Nabisco, Willie T. said nothing. The first week, Gar made a few comments, but soon he gave up and kept quiet, forgot the whole thing. Each time Willie T. saw something new about the van. A cracked taillight held a pocket of brown water, the left rear fender bent in above the rusting brake. A decal on the front bumper read, "Trust in the Lord"; the state plates said, "Oklahoma is OK."

At work Willie T. ran the salter with his usual touch, but he thought constantly of the van, of retirement, and after. As the grids of steaming crackers rolled beneath him, he bled salt from the hopper with the clutch, the rotor under his seat growling like a four-barrel.

When Willie T. called at coffee break, a salesman told him the van cost two thousand dollars. Willie T. thought it was low because of the bashed-in rear. No problem: Beatty, an old friend who owned a garage, could bang out the quarter-panel and straighten the wheel. He'd have to buy a new tire and a new rim, that was only two or three hundred. Still, they didn't have that much in the bank, and even if they did, Christine would never let him spend all of it.

A loan would do it, but before he could think about a loan he had to see what jobs were open. He spent Sunday afternoon at the dinner table leafing through the classifieds. Christine, watching an old movie on TV, glanced over from time to time. He pretended it was the sports pages, grumbling, "Rangers trying to sign that fat boy Gedman. Says Herschel wants two million next year." She waved her hand, shooing his comments.

For all his searching, he found only one opportunity. "Personal Transit," it read, "Individual to transport small treatment group." He neatly tore the ad out and tucked it in his wallet.

He called Monday. "Sunrise Home," a woman answered, "I'll connect you with personnel, please hold." Buzzing, then a man came on. "Yes?"

Four hundred a month, the man said. Noise from the floor made it hard to hear him. Two trips a day, five days a week, six patients per trip. Willie T. wanted to ask what kind of patients, then figured it didn't matter. If they were crazy or dangerous they wouldn't have advertised in the paper. The end of break bell rang, and the foreman stalked into the vending machine room. "What type of vehicle do you own?" the man asked.

Willie T. lied.

"Am I correct in assuming you have a carrier's license and the proper insurance?"

Willie T. lied again. The foreman began throwing away coffee cups. Smokers ground their cigarettes out and scattered. "I got to go now," Willie T. said, "but it sounds real good. Thanks a lot." He put his hard hat on and snuck back to the salter, where he dreamt away the rest of the morning, gliding over a fragrant highway of saltines.

On the way home, stopped beneath the blue and white Way-noka Ford sign, Willie T. swore out loud. Gar had left work early for a dentist's appointment, so there was no one to hem Willie T. in. He stood in the lot, looking at the van, despairing. The loan, the job, it was all too complicated. The risk was too great. They'd been poor before, but they were young then, and work came easier. License, insurance, tax. He was no closer to owning the van now than when he first saw it; it was all an old fool's daydream.

He stepped to the driver's side, opened the door and climbed in. Worn smooth, the oversized wheel fit his hands. The interior smelled of stale cigarettes and grease; on the dash lay a squadron of dead flies, stiff-legged. Willie T. gripped the wheel, shifted his butt on the seat, and pumped the pedals. He twisted around and tested the first bench seat. The upholstery sprang back when he bounced. He slid the panel door open, got out, shut it, slid it open again and shut it again. He knelt, took a penny from his pocket and checked the tire treads, then lay on his back and inspected the undercarriage for rust. Everything looked fine.

A man in a suit and tie came out of the showroom doors. Willie T. waved, and the man began to thread his way toward him through the maze of parked cars. He was short, fat, and white, and his suit was too small for him. Red socks flashed as he approached. They met and shook hands.

"Floyd Bannister," the man said, "glad to meet you. I see you've been looking over this Ford here. It's a fine machine." His hands flew as he spoke. "Interested?"

"Might be," Willie T. said. "The man last week said it's two thousand."

"That's correct."

"Even with the back messed up?"

The man surveyed the damage, scratching his jaw. "We could fix her for you, but that would kick the price up considerably." His hand stopped, a finger pointing to the sky.

"I don't know. It looks like a lot of work."

"Why don't we go inside, Mr. Tillman? Let's see what it looks like on paper."

When Willie T. left, it was dark. He felt his way through the lot, guided by the liquid shimmer of fenders, hoods, and windows. Beyond the lot flames shot from the refinery's safety valves. "Thursday," Floyd Bannister called, "don't forget now."

After Willie T. finished his speech, Christine wiped her mouth with her napkin, replaced it in her lap, and rested her arms on the table, one on each side of her plate. She stared at him as if decided, features set, eyes searching his.

"So?" he asked.

"I knew you been scheming on something, I knew it." She looked at the ceiling, puffed her cheeks full of air, then let it out.

"You're gonna quit your job and drive around in this van all day. And the money they pay is gonna keep us alive. On top of the pension and Social Security."

"Four hundred dollars, way more —"

"Wait." She held up a hand. "You're not gonna be home most of the time now, getting in my way?" He nodded. "Then OK. It's crazy, but OK, go ahead. At least you're finally thinking about retiring and what we're gonna do." He scooted around the table and hugged her in her chair. "Long as you aren't home all the time," she said, holding his arms against her chest. "I don't want no shadow hanging around."

That night, he woke in darkness, suddenly, as if from a nightmare. An arm of light stretched gray across the ceiling. What if he failed? Christine's breathing filled the room. He lay his head on the mattress and held the pillow close against his ear. In the silence, he heard his own breath, and growing steadily, like footsteps, the beating of his heart.

The next day at work he called the Sunrise Home to see if the job was still open. The man he had spoken to before said it was and asked him when he could start. Willie T. told him he didn't know. Soon. The line was silent, then the man said, "To be honest, we haven't been getting much of a response. If you can come up with something in a few weeks, I suppose we can struggle through with what we have." Willie T. gave him all the information. When he got off the phone, he clapped his hands together once and said, "Yeah!" The smokers turned their heads for a second, then went on smoking.

Coming home, Willie T. said to Gar, "I'm gonna buy that van." Gar began to say something, but Willie T. kept on, "I'm gonna buy that van and haul people around in it." He kicked a stone with his boot and it skittered across the road. "Don't tell me I won't, cause I will."

Gar stopped and looked at him. "You've been up to something." He smiled, then nodded solemnly. "I believe you, Willie T., I believe you're gonna buy that van."

"I'm gonna have something for when I retire, see?"

"Guess so."

"What are you gonna have?"

Gar shrugged. "I got some years to go yet."

"It's something to think on. Cause I been thinking on it, and let me tell you, if you're old they let you starve. They throw you out in the street if they like, and that's no lie." He turned and walked, and Gar followed.

Thursday after work he met with Floyd Bannister and gave him a check for four hundred dollars. The two thousand now included licensing, registration, a ten-month warranty on the engine, and a tow to the garage. By the time Beatty fixed the left rear, Willie T. would be in business. Which worked out well, considering he had to give Nabisco two weeks notice. The deal was running so smoothly that Willie T. got nervous. Pen in hand, he imagined accidents, thieves, and after he signed, walking home, not even the van itself, tilting on its cinder block, could cheer him.

"Wonderful," the man from the Sunrise Home said. "Send us a copy of your papers, and we'll draft a contract here. If you can get us the paperwork this week, we'll have the contract back to you next Wednesday or Thursday."

"Sounds good," Willie T. said. Gar made faces at him, held out a palm to slap.

"Very good, Mr. Tillman. We look forward to hearing from you."

He thought he would love leaving Nabisco. He and Christine had agreed that he could quit. Having served over twenty-five years, he would retire at full pension. Gar congratulated him daily, and they joked about it, but the last two weeks were hard on Willie T. Friends he hadn't seen in years dropped by to wish him luck. "Don't forget us now," they said. On his last Friday, the department threw a party for him, with free coffee and a cake from the cafeteria. His foreman made a speech praising Willie T.'s initiative, thanking him for his long service. Gar presented him with a pair of leather driving gloves on behalf of the crew. "Speech,

speech," everyone said. Willie T. held the gloves up and said, "Thanks, everybody." The room filled with laughter, applause.

The sun setting, Gar and Willie T. passed Waynoka Ford. The cinder block sat in an empty space. They walked the refinery fence and up onto the bridge, boots crunching in the gritty dirt, lunch pails swinging, squeaking. The refrigerator shone dully from the riverbed. Silent, they went by the Arco, Big Ed's, and the bowling alley and came to Gar's corner. "All right, Willie T., you come back and see us sometime." He shook Willie T.'s hand.

"I will, Gar." They broke, Gar heading down his street, Willie T. crossing. As he was walking away, Willie T. paused and looked back. Gar's brown jacket glided through the circle below a street-light, then vanished into darkness, appeared again, vanished again, and on down the street, smaller and smaller.

Saturday morning Willie T. arrived at Beatty's Garage before Beatty did. The van sat in the parking lot, surrounded by wrecks. Above a new tire, a coat of gray primer covered the left rear fender. "Looking good," Willie T. said, smoothing the paint with his hand.

He found a pay phone and called the Sunrise Home. "I'll be ready Monday," he told the man. "What time you want me there?"

"That's fine, Mr. Tillman. We'll expect you at ten o'clock. We have to go over the terms of the contract, and that will take an hour or so. Then at eleven you have a group going to the Care Center, and their return trip at two. So, yes, we'll be looking for you around ten."

"Sounds good."

Beatty showed up an hour later. Willie T. paid him with a check and picked up the keys. They went out to the van and Willie T. started it. "I took it out yesterday," Beatty said, leaning against the door. "It runs pretty steady. There's some little things, some touch-up work, but overall it's solid." The engine rumbled, the wheel tingled in Willie T.'s hands. "If anything goes wrong, bring it back in and I'll take care of it."

"Hey, Beatty, it's a help, man."

"No trouble." He smacked the door. "Drive on, Willie T."

He had driven a van in the fifties when he worked at Hoover's Laundry, but now, easing the Econoline through the narrow streets of Waynoka, Willie T. felt as if he were no longer part of traffic. He drove slowly, gauging the van's size, looping wide on turns, braking early. He took it out on Route 64 and raced it one exit, turned around and raced it back. Before going home, he stopped for gas. He pulled up to the full service island and had the attendant fill the tank and check all the fluids. Inspired, he drove to the Self-Wash and sprayed and vacuumed for an hour. The windows threw rays. He climbed in, removed the box with Gar's gloves from the dash, pulled the gloves on and started home, whistling.

Christine looked it over, nodding. "You're right, it's a real nice van." She walked around it. "You gonna take me for a ride, Mr. Bus Driver?" Willie T. kissed her, opened the passenger door and helped her up onto the seat. She ran her hand over the vinyl, touched the invisible windows. "It really is something," she said.

They drove all Saturday afternoon and most of Sunday, testing the Econoline. He slipped between lines of cars stopped at lights, changed lanes without turning his head. Christine sat in the middle of the rear bench seat, and Willie T. practiced driving with passengers.

Monday he woke at the regular time and tried to go back to sleep, but it was useless. He took a shower, shaved, dressed in his best work clothes, ate breakfast, then read the paper until nine. The Sunrise Home was on the other edge of town, only twenty minutes away, but he didn't want to be late. He left at 9:15. Christine pecked him on the cheek and gave him his lunch bag. "Drive safe now," she called from the door.

Mr. Binstock, the man he had spoken with on the phone, seemed smaller in person, but just as courteous. After signing the contract, he led Willie T. around the complex, pointing out the residential wing, the medical facilities, the recreation unit. Old people in lemon yellow sweaters wandered the lawns and hedge-lined paths. "Our residents," Mr. Binstock lectured, "receive the finest care available. I trust you will maintain a professional atti-tude, and at all times the state of your vehicle must be immacu-late. Remember, only the finest." A woman tottered by, mumbling to herself. "As you well see, some of our residents may require a bit of extra understanding. I think we can both agree that this is important. At our age, Mr. Tillman, I believe we should realize how critical that special touch is, don't you?"

Willie T. noticed that all of the residents were white. Strangely, none rolled in wheelchairs or leaned on walkers or hobbled on canes. They strolled along in their matching lemon sweaters, tanned faces beaming. A country club, Willie T. thought.

The six an orderly helped into his van were no exception. He checked their names against a list Mr. Binstock had given him. They shifted across the seats, greeting him with rearviewed waves. The man directly behind him laid his hand on Willie T.'s shoulder and whispered, "Glad you finally showed. That damn station wagon was kicking the hell out of us."

"Yes, sir." Willie T. laughed.

The orderly slid the door shut, and Willie T. pulled away. Taped to the dash, the instructions to the Care Center trembled. At the front gate he pressed them against the dashboard to read them. His passengers chatted, a steady murmur softening the thrum of the engine. He turned left across traffic, swinging her in a long arc. No one complained.

The ride lasted half an hour. South out of town along 281, through prairie, horse-head rigs, and power lines; then east on 15, with the tankers on their way to Enid. They crossed the Cimar-ron River twice. Willie T. kept to the right, the needle on 55. Be-hind him, his passengers laughed and hollered over the highway wind. He changed lanes before exits, avoiding on-ramps.

The Care Center, a poured concrete block banded by mirrored windows, sat in the suburbs of Cleo Springs. Willie T. cruised

around a circular drive and stopped in front of a group of uni-
formed orderlies. While they helped his passengers out, he took
off Gar's gloves, pulled out a map and drew the route on it in
Magic Marker. One of the orderlies came over to his window and
said, "So you're the new guy. My name's Eddie." His hand reached
in over the map.

"Willie T."

"We should be done around 1:30, so get yourself a coffee and
be back by a quarter past, all right, Willie T.?"

On the return trip, one of his passengers, a fat woman with
clear orange barrettes, threw up. Willie T. saw her in the rearview
mirror, a consoling arm across her bent back. Terrified, he found
a wide part of the shoulder, pulled off and stopped.

"Don't worry," the man behind him said, "it's only Clara. She'll
be fine when we get home."

Willie T. sat staring at his lined, gray face.

"I'll take care of everything," the man said, "you just keep driving." He took a handkerchief from his pants pocket, rose from his
seat and made his way to the woman. "Go on," he waved, "drive."

Moving again, Willie T. watched him open a window and drop
the handkerchief out. "All set, Ace," the man called, smiling. Back
in his seat, he whispered, "I think you'd better invest in a slop jar.
Clara's pretty regular."

After rinsing the floor at the Self-Wash, Willie T. bought a
plastic bucket at the Savemore. When Christine asked him how
his day went, he didn't mention it. "Bunch of rich old people," he
said. "It's a breeze."

The next day it happened again, but this time the bucket saved
the floor. They rode with the windows open, and on his way home
Willie T. bought a hanging air freshener.

Aside from Clara's vomiting, the week went well. Willie T.
knew their names and as much about them as their conversations
allowed. The man behind him was their unofficial leader, Mr.
Fergus. To his right sat Mr. DiSilvio, and in the seat nearest the

door, Mr. Johns. Behind them sat the girls: on the left, Mrs. Ryerson, by the window, Miss Flynn, and in the middle, fussed over, the baby, Clara.

The hours were good, the pay was good, and the work was easy. Emptying the bucket every day was nothing compared to Nabisco, and although he hadn't said much yet, he imagined he'd like talking with his passengers. They seemed nice. He would have felt sorry for them, being in a home, but they didn't act sad, so why should he? In fact, as the week went on, Willie T. began to envy them. He was sixty-two, and before he took the job he worried about growing old, losing it. But listening to Mr. Fergus describe smuggling gin in a flower vase, he forgot about age. Or to see Mrs. Ryerson and Miss Flynn patting Clara on the back, soothing her. At Nabisco, Willie T. thought sixty-five was the end. It worried him that Christine was all the family he had, that he was all she had. Knowing there would always be someone like Mr. Fergus, or even Mr. DiSilvio, let Willie T. sleep easier.

Saturday at the Self-Wash, Willie T. swept a handful of hair out the door. He held it up, the sky showing through the loose wool. "Guess something's got to go," he said. It floated to the ground and the wind rolled it away.

The second Monday he drove a different route, taking the hilly back roads. The group cheered each dip and curve. Every day he found a new combination, and by the end of the week Mr. Fergus was guiding them to the Care Center, crinkling the map, tapping Willie T.'s shoulder right or left. Mr. Johns wondered if the radio was broken. They rode, lost, Benny Goodman and the Dorsey brothers swinging, Mr. Johns snapping the time. Stepping down, the girls said, "Good-night, Mr. Tillman."

Nabisco officially shut down at five-thirty on Fridays, but no one stayed that late. Willie T. waited outside the fence, beside the guardhouse, secretly thrilled. It felt like playing hooky. Around five, cars started escaping, speeding at first, then creeping along as the guard stopped traffic to let other workers cross. Gar walked down the middle of the vacant entry lane, shaking his lunch pail at the cars, calling "Have a good one. All right, you too." Willie T. honked the horn to get his attention.

They chose The Wildcat over Big Ed's because it had free pork rinds and the jukebox played the old songs. Beer raised, Gar toasted Willie T. "To the millionaire." They clinked mugs and drank. "Really, sounds like my kind of job. Get up late, don't do much of nothing, quit early. Yeah, sounds mighty sweet."

"It's like I told you, Gar, you got to be thinking 'bout these things."

"Yeah, well." He sipped. "I'm doing all right for myself." He rolled the mug in his hands, set it down. "C'mon, let's spin some tunes."

Sweeping that Saturday, Willie T. formed a hairball the size of a grapefruit. He brushed his hands over the seats; a sparse fur clung to them. He paid fifty cents for a vacuum and did the interior.

After dropping them off Monday, he asked Eddie why there was so much hair.

"It's just a side effect," Eddie told him. "Sometimes it's worse, and their teeth fall out too. Some puke. From what I can tell, it's almost as bad as the cancer. I mean, what's the difference? No one really gets any better. Hey, want to see the place?" he asked. "There's some wild stuff."

"I don't know."

"C'mon, you can leave the van here, it's safe."

"That's all right. I got to get my coffee."

On the return trip, he joked with Mr. Fergus, played the radio for Mr. Johns, and told Clara everything was fine; but that night, in bed, all he could think of was death. He didn't want to worry Christine, so he lay awake, dreading morning and the van, their doomed smiles in the mirror.

While Christine showered, he called in sick. He left the apartment at nine, but instead of heading for work, he drove to Woods

County Courthouse and searched the bulletin boards for job notices. There were none. He called Personnel at Nabisco. Finally he stopped at Waynoka Ford and talked with Floyd Bannister. There was no way back without losing money or the van or both. He filled the tank at a self-serve and drove away the afternoon, cruising the unknown streets south of town.

The next morning Mr. Fergus asked him if he was feeling better. Willie T. said he was. At lunch he bought a paper and looked through the classifieds. The schools wanted drivers but supplied their own vans. Other than that there was nothing.

As the days passed, he grew desperate. He was sure one of them would die soon, merely because he knew they had it. He scanned the classifieds and bulletin boards for the one opening that would free him.

Week after week he drove, and soon he stopped searching for another job. The shock worn off, he blamed himself for overreacting. They would outlive him. While they were with him in the van he could think like this, but at night the fear returned.

Then Mr. DiSilvio began to fade. His skin broke out in blotches, rust-brown lesions crusted with an ointment the Home's doctor prescribed. On hot days it soaked through his shirt like grease. He spoke less, and when he did, he complained. Mr. Fergus's jokes fell in silence. Mr. Johns ignored Glenn Miller. The girls sat tight-lipped in back, their eyes pleading with the mirror. He still hadn't told Christine.

Night again. Willie T. recited, held a shield of words. He could quit and Nabisco would rehire him. He could sell the van at a loss. He could drive for the schools and sell the van at a loss. He could quit. They would die one by one, and he would drive the empty van to the Care Center and tell Eddie, "Nothing today," and drive back. Mr. Johns would be the last, his big bands blaring from the speakers, a trio of singers in matching skirts and hairdos swaying, soldiers on leave dancing with USO girls. The light gauzy with cigarette smoke, a clarinet snaked through to Mr. Johns, buckled in his seat, staring past Willie T. into the onrushing dark. The dark where Willie T. lay, breath roaring.

The lesions grew worse. The orderlies struggled to fit his hunched body into his seat. In the new silence he sometimes moaned, low, drawn out sighs of pain. Willie T. kept his eyes on the road.

He worried about the others. Grim, they sat in their places each day while Mr. DiSilvio paled and worsened, the lesions spreading, joining like glaciers. His moans rose in pitch, trailed off like echoes. The ointment stank. Willie T. drove, imagining them asleep in bed, alone, the black of the Sunrise Home broken by the nurse's call buzzer, the muffled rush of rubber soles. Trays, needles. When they woke, the room across the hall would be empty, an orderly's mop sloshing.

At the end of Willie T.'s first three months, Mr. Binstock called him into his office for an evaluation. A manila folder lay open on his desk. He flipped through it, stabbing facts with his eraser. "Yes . . . yes . . . yes." Willie T. sat straight in the chair, kneading Gar's stiff gloves. Now was his chance to quit. The six were safely home, the van waited by the curb, ready for a getaway. He wouldn't have to see them ever again. Or if Mr. Binstock gave him a poor review. Mr. Binstock closed the folder. "Excellent, Mr. Tillman, positively excellent. Punctual, courteous, mindful of our residents' needs. Despite your relative inexperience, your work here is coming along fine. We are prepared to offer you a permanent position here at Sunrise, at a competitive wage, of course." Willie T. nodded, staring at the gloves. They were curled and hard, like shells. "I'm sure your decision will take some consideration. Regardless, you may expect an increase in your check beginning this month." He rose and stretched a hand toward Willie T.

Willie T. rose and shook it. "Thanks a lot."

"Keep up the good work." Mr. Binstock smiled.

They were five that Friday. Mr. Binstock gave Willie T. a new passenger list. The orderlies helped them in, and Willie T. pulled away. No one spoke. In the mirror, Mr. DiSilvio's safety belt lay on the vinyl seat. Willie T. eased left across traffic.

When they came to the intersection where Mr. Fergus made his first navigator's decision, Willie T. waited for the tap on his shoulder, but it never came. The light changed, and he drove straight ahead. The next light was green. He slowed, waiting for Mr. Fergus to choose, but again, nothing, and he pressed the gas pedal. South out of town along 281, across the Cimarron, then east on 15, and across again. Mr. Johns didn't ask for the radio.

Eddie said, "You can't get involved. They come in and they leave and sometimes they don't come back. You gotta get used to it, otherwise you might as well sell this thing."

Clara threw up on the return trip. Willie T. heard her, but didn't look back. 15 west, the river, 281 north, the river, and into Waynoka. They were quiet for a while, and he raised his eyes to the mirror. Above their bright sweaters gray skin sagged, eyes red pouches, cheeks scarred and folded. Scalp shone through Mr. Johns's remaining hair, through Mr. Fergus's. Willie T. met his own eyes and drove on.

He stayed in Saturday and Sunday and watched the Rangers beat the Yanks twice. The classifieds lay untouched on the dining room table. He sank into his stuffed chair and let the tide of ball-strike counts wash over him. He knew he could not last. He would sell the van and go back to Nabisco. Outside, Sunday afternoon bled into Sunday night, the threat of Monday caught in long, reaching shadows.

In the morning they were six again, Mr. DiSilvio's seat filled by Mr. Paulsen, a short, wide man with no hair. The attendants buckled everyone in and slid the door shut, and Willie T. coasted the Econoline down the drive. Behind him, Mr. Fergus told the newcomer a dirty joke. The girls tittered despite themselves. "Really, Mr. Fergus," Miss Flynn scolded. Mr. Johns sat staring blankly, his hands folded in his lap. The river twice. From time to time Willie T. glanced hopefully in the mirror. Mr. Fergus had the girls leaning forward to hear his punch lines. In the aisle seat Mr. Johns still sagged, resigned. Mr. Paulsen hooted, the girls giggled. Willie T. steered the van into the Care Center's drive. A line of orderlies stood at the curb, legs apart, hands behind, heads raised as if for inspection. In the late morning sun their white uniforms shone. Like angels, Willie T. thought, like angels at-ease.

While the orderlies helped the six out, Eddie came over to Willie T.'s window. "How you doing, Willie T.?"

"Getting along, how about you?"

"Can't complain. Just wanted to see how things are."

"Hanging in there," Willie T. said, but he was lying. The rest of the week he and Mr. Johns rode together, separated from the others by silence. He swore he could smell Mr. DiSilvio's ointment. Like horseradish, or ammonia.

Mr. Paulsen roared at Mr. Fergus's jokes and told some of his own. Mr. Johns loomed in the mirror, his face gray, his eyes set. Willie T. drove.

He explained it to Christine. She thought he should quit. "It's not good," she said. "You're gonna end up like them, not knowing when to laugh or cry." Their discussions lasted through dinner, TV, all the way to bed. But Christine was a regular sleeper, and each night her words stopped in the dark, left Willie T. alone, adrift.

The next Thursday Mr. Binstock asked Willie T. to see him in his office after the return trip. He knocked on the door. "Yes?" said Mr. Binstock. Sitting across from him, Mr. Fergus turned to watch Willie T. Have a seat, Mr. Binstock gestured.

"Mr. Tillman," Mr. Binstock began, "We have a serious problem here. Mr. Fergus has informed me that you are not happy. Need I tell you how important it is for someone in your position to project a positive attitude? That is one reason why Mr. Fergus accompanies your group — to keep them happy."

Mr. Fergus nodded at Willie T.

Mr. Binstock continued: "At first your work was fine; excellent, in fact. But there was no reason why it wouldn't be. Now, when you should be the most supportive, you mope through your duties. Do you understand what I'm saying?"

"Yes, sir, but they're dying. How'm I—"

"Mr. Tillman," Mr. Fergus interrupted, "you don't have to stop them from dying, or even thinking about dying. All you have to do—what I do—is help them enjoy living."

"You see," Mr. Binstock said, "when someone knows they're dying, they're apt to refuse to live."

"Like Mr. Johns," Mr. Fergus added.

"Exactly," Mr. Binstock said. "But all you have to do in that situation is stress how enjoyable life is. There's nothing sadder than people who give up and simply wait. Like our Mr. Johns. As you've seen, the others are in no better shape. Physically, that is. Mentally they're far healthier."

Willie T. looked at Gar's gloves, turning them over and over.

"You can do a lot," Mr. Fergus said, touching Willie T.'s arm. "Start with the radio. Talk, swear at the other drivers—anything. We can pull Mr. Johns out of this."

"Some of these people are going to die," Mr. Binstock said. "But they can do more than sit around and wait for it." He paused, waiting for Willie T. to respond, then said, "Next month I'll be asking you to join our fulltime staff. I thought I should inform you of our philosophy."

Willie T. said nothing.

"All right then, that's all."

That night over dinner, Willie T. told Christine about Mr. Fergus. "Like a spy," she said. "I guess he's right though. Makes a lot of sense, really. Think of that! It'd make you more important than any old bus driver."

After she fell asleep, Willie T. worked out what was right, what was possible and what he would do. Before work the next day he washed and vacuumed the van. At work, driving, he spoke with his passengers and sang along with the radio. For two weeks he did this, and with the help of Mr. Fergus and the natural cheer of Mr. Paulsen, Mr. Johns returned to his normal self.

But even as his passengers laughed and joked, Willie T. never forgot they were going to die. Acting as if there was nothing wrong was easier than believing it. Christine was proud of him, Mr. Binstock was proud of him, Mr. Fergus was proud of him. To fight their combined respect, regardless of the money, would have been stupid. So he drove, terrified, unbelieving.

Sometimes when the radio played a certain song, or when Mr. Johns tried to scat with Ella Fitzgerald, or when Mr. Fergus got the girls giggling, Willie T. could believe. An automatic moment which, appreciated, vanished immediately. He smelled the ointment, saw the shirt translucent as waxed paper, the blotches spreading like spilled wine. "Everything's OK," he told Eddie. "Work was fine," he told Christine. "Looking good," he told Mr. Binstock. But he could not fool Mr. Fergus.

One summer day, after the return trip, Mr. Fergus dismissed the orderly and stayed in his seat. "Where to?" Willie T. joked.

"You're scared, Mr. Tillman. I can tell. It's in your eyes, it's in your voice. I've seen it before, I know what I'm seeing."

"These people are dying and I'm supposed to be glad all the time?"

"Here," Mr. Fergus said, shoving his arm over the seat. Below his wrist a red sore burned like a star, and below it, another. On the inside of his elbow yellow skin ringed deep blue bruises. "You don't have to be scared, Mr. Tillman. No one has to be scared." He withdrew his arm and rolled the sleeve of his Sunrise sweater over it. Then he held up both hands, fingers splayed apart, and smiled. "See? All gone." He showed Willie T. the palms and backs like a magician. "Nothing to be afraid of, right?"

Willie T. shook his head. "I'm sorry."

"Don't be, there's no reason. Think of it this way: when you see something coming, you get ready for it. You plan around it. Most people worry about when it's going to come. Christ, that's what kills half the people here."

Willie T. did not want to be in the van with Mr. Fergus. He was thinking of the salter and coffee break and walking with Gar. Mr. Fergus faded in and out. He was trying to give Willie T. something.

"So we'll look at it tomorrow, all right? Mr. Tillman?"

"I don't want nothing." He turned away and hid behind the headrest.

"You'll need it, Mr. Tillman. Believe me, you'll need it."

"I don't want it, I don't want anything."

Mr. Fergus patted his shoulder. "You get some rest. We'll talk tomorrow."

After work the next day, while the others tottered back to their rooms, Mr. Fergus stayed in his seat. "We can do it today or we can do it tomorrow," he said. "It's up to you."

Except for his meetings with Mr. Binstock, Willie T. had never seen the inside of the Sunrise Home. He followed Mr. Fergus down stucco hallways, across bright linoleum floors. They turned a corner and passed the curved counter of a nurses' station. The rooms were open, and inside, residents sat in groups, playing cards on hospital beds. In a darkened room an air-conditioner hummed. Mr. Fergus stopped, opened a door and let Willie T. enter first.

Black-and-white photographs of Mr. Fergus covered the walls. Dancing in tails, a cane and tophat held in flying hands. As a hobo, fondling a huge bottle of moonshine. Willie T. thought he recognized a young Bob Hope. As he went from wall to wall, Mr. Fergus rummaged through a dirty kitchenette. Harry James, Mae West, Groucho. A framed playbill signed by the cast of "South Pacific."

"Didn't know I was famous, did you?" Mr. Fergus thumped a cardboard box down on a coffee table and waved Willie T. over. "I still sell a gag once in a while. Only to the big guys, the new stuff's beyond me." He popped the lid off the box; inside sat a stack of paper. Mr. Fergus riffled the stack. "These I've never used, not really anyway. You got your blue material, your one-liners and rim shots, heckler put-downs, wife routines." He pointed to a rainbow of section dividers. "Your drunk jokes, your moron jokes, your New York and L.A. jokes. Let's see, fat, ugly, Irish — you got to laugh at yourself, right?— Black, Polish, Italian, Jews. You got Democrat stuff, Republican stuff, hippies, rednecks, animal bits. You got it all."

He patted the stack and looked at Willie T. "Remember, anyone can be funny. You practice hard enough, you can be really funny. But it's in here that makes a comedian a comedian. Because you can't make fun of people. You've got to give them room. I've seen people with great material bomb, not because they didn't know people, but because they didn't like people. And you like people, Mr. Tillman. That's why you need this, that's why I'm giving it to you."

Willie T. took the box and the lid and fit them together. It was obvious to him that Mr. Fergus was crazy. "Thanks a lot," he said, tucking the box under his arm and backing away. "I'll be seeing you tomorrow."

Mr. Fergus followed him out, calling after him, "Don't forget, Mr. Tillman, it's all in here."

"I got you," Willie T. called back.

He hid the box under an old pair of boots in the bedroom closet.

The following weeks Mr. Fergus seemed fine. He told his jokes and laughed at Mr. Paulsen's, slapped the back of Willie T.'s seat when Mr. Johns sang. He did a play-by-play of Clara's vomiting and teased Mrs. Ryerson and Miss Flynn about their new summer wigs. But Willie T. knew he didn't have long. His sleeves came to his wrists, and the smell of ointment grew so strong that even on the rare cool mornings Willie T. kept the windows open.

Soon the orderly had to lift him from his seat and carry him out the door. He arrived early each day so the others wouldn't see him, and when they left he stayed in his seat and talked with Willie T. until the orderly wheeled the chair to the curb. He spoke of his childhood, his adventures as a young man, his career, his marriages. History poured out of him. Willie T. tried not to judge. As Mr. Fergus grew weaker, his ramblings took in his whole life. One minute he'd be talking about the wharves in Brooklyn, the next the rotten food in the cafeteria. He repeated episodes and forgot important details, and yet he seemed to be concentrating, correcting himself, as if every new version were the last and had to be perfect. Willie T. never interrupted. He told himself that the urgency in Mr. Fergus's voice was natural.

And one August morning they were five again. They crossed the river south, the river east, silent. He told Eddie how brave Mr. Fergus was.

After dinner, Christine left Willie T. to himself. He sat in his stuffed chair and drank beer, ignoring the TV, and by bedtime he was drunk. Christine turned off all the lights and asked, "You coming?"

"In a while."

The beer was warm and sour going down. He slouched in the chair, the blue ghosts of the TV racing around the walls. He went to the kitchen for another beer, came back and watched the ceiling flow. It was two o'clock when he finished the last one, the national anthem long past, the screen a blur of grinding static.

Barefoot, he crept into the dark bedroom. The closet door squeaked. He dug through boots and shoes to the box. In the living room the glare of the TV flashed like summer lightning over the walls. He flicked the bathroom switch, set the box on the toilet, and sat down on the lip of the tub. A grainy Mr. Fergus smiled up at him. Willie T. took the first sheet from the box, held it above the sink, and began to read. In the mirror his lips moved, his voice soft in the cold, tiled light, murmuring as if in prayer.